Ghetto Luv

Mary L. Wilson

Published by Prioritybooks Publications
Missouri

Prioritybooks Publications
P.O. Box 2535
Florissant, Mo 63033

Manufactured in the United States of America

Library of Congress Control Number
2005909496

ISBN 0-9753634-3-3

Cover designed by Inkosidesigns
Edited by Diane Page

For information regarding discounts for bulk purchases, please contact Prioritybooks Publications at 1-314-741-6789 or marylwilson2003@yahoo.com or mail to P. O. Box 5036, St. Louis, MO 63115. You may also email rosbeav03@yahoo.com.

Ghetto Luv

Acknowledgements

I give all admiration and praises to the Creator above for blessing me with a vision. Without a vision, we would perish. Lacking your wisdom and knowledge, I am nobody. Everything is promised because you sacrificed your life for me, and I am most thankful and delighted that you chose me.

Mama, Patricia Hatton, thank you for instilling Christ in my life at an early age. I love you for your enduring support. Anitra, my princess, thank you for the title to this book. Antonio, my king, education is the key to success, and a mind is a terrible thing to waste, so keep spitting those rhymes. Manuel, my king, I know you're going to be the next Michael Jordan. There are no words to illustrate the love I have for the three of you. Thanks for the tremendous support that you all have contributed while on my journey. I'll never fail to remember the comedy shows in the living room.

My little sister but big sister, Tammie Wilson, maintain the superior effort that you're putting forth in school and the magnificent job you're doing raising my two nieces, Tandra and Latrice. They are the most precious girls I have ever seen. TeTe, love ya'll. My brother, Lamont, keep doing what you do. You're going to be on someone's record label real soon. Jermon, my baby brother, those computers work for you, baby. Thanks for assisting your big sister whenever I needed you. Jerline and Evelyn, I am most thankful to have you two as aunts—the best that any person could have. I wouldn't trade you all for anything in this world.

Curfrances (Shorty-Curt) Wright, my best friend and my big sister—girl, you need to be on comic view, because you tell it like it really is. That's why I love you. Without your nineteen years of friendship, I don't know what I would have done sometimes. Friends like you come once in a lifetime, and I value every minute of yours. To my goddaughter, Janise Brooks, slow down, caramel beauty. Frances Wright, thank you for inventing my best friend. Mannie, keep your head up. The McKinney family: Curtis, Betty, Tasha, Mya, Mary, Kesha, Crystal, Frankie and "Fatman Rip," I express much thanks for your support.

Coco, you know you should have been my brother instead of my cousin, but I love you for what you are. Shonesia, do you, girl. Vershell, it's hard being you. Lisa, gotta love you. Tasha, keep it movin'.

To the rest of my family, which includes so many of us—Chris, Pat, Shantae, Jig, Ricky, Kim, Tina, Will, Marco, Tona, Red, Glitter, Pam, Minnie, Diane, Doris, Brenda, June Bug, Terry, Fee, Lil James, Anthony, Meka, April Do, Donyale, Dominque, Rico, Troy, Jessica, Marilyn, Squeaky, DJ, Reggie, Crystal, Shane, Sheila and the others who are not mentioned, thank you. Sharkira (Coopie Ray) Wilson, you are in a class all by yourself, lady.

To the Hendrix Family: Denise, we need to be private investigators. Theresa, when I think of you, a smile immediately crosses my face. Latrice, Paula, Doris, Rose, Lamar and Donald, I don't know where to begin to thank you. Friends are forever. May God continue to bless all of you, as well as your families.

To the Crossland family: My dog, my dirty, my partner in crime, Tonya (Bad Feet) Crossland, I love you, girl. Thanks for reading my book first and for keeping it so real. And thanks most of all for allowing me to set up my office in the corner of your house. (Smile!)

Tanesha Baker, thanks for being my editor, big girl. Continue to remain on honor roll. Nichole, Anthony, Lil Harold, Antwon, Mike, Manuel, Ebony, daddy Ricky and Lil Sam, you know it's a Libra thang. Rhonda, thanks for coming through when I needed you the most. Papa, you know I love you, Baby Love. Annie Bea, thanks a million for the pep talks.

To the hood: Keke, Pooh, Mark, Mike, Bric, Shonda, Precious, Joann, Max, Bo, Ozzie, Vinny, Chuck, Dre, Keith, Bay Bay, Big Dre and Lawanda, and to the Yates-Johnson Family: Aubrey, Quentin, Lil Man, Audrey, Quana, Ciara and Pam, thank you.

Kelly, I didn't fail to remember you, baby, or Pamela Madison. You all were my strength so many times in the past. God puts different people in your life for different reasons, and I'm glad he blessed me with you two!

Tiffany Ross, you are my girl, and I appreciate you more than you'll ever know. Lisa Roberson and Terria Greenlee, we can sit around for hours and converse about a book. Thanks for the discussion and suggestions.

The McClendon Family: Mrs. Daisy, you're the woman. Byrd, Michelle, Tate, Tilly, Rene and all the kids, thanks for your good cooking and fun. My baby, Archie, I never knew genuine love until I met you. You have sustained me from day one. Thank you for everything you have done for me. I'm astonished when I think of your unrestricted love for me.

We did it! Mr. Brown, I can remember telling you I wanted to be a writer, and you told me to go for it. Thanks for believing in me and giving me my real first job. Mrs. Brown Wilson, we did it!

Mrs. Beavers, thank you for the opportunity to characterize myself as a conqueror. You came along just when I wanted to revolve into another course and escorted me without delay. You are a blessing, and I can't thank you enough.

To the Jackson family: "Linda aka Mom," thank you for demonstrating how a lady presents herself and for being a fraction of my life. Big Tony, I did it! Monesia, you are always there when I want to vent. There are no words that can express my gratitude. Kiss Chance,

Symoria and Tia for me. I love you a whole bunch.
Teressa and Shonda thanks for keeping my hair looking
gorgeous. Special thanks to the Bright family.

Everyone who said I couldn't do it, look at me now!
And to all my haters, you know who you are. Picture me
rollin', and please believe I did brush my shoulders off! I
made it do what it do, baby!

On a more serious note, dreams do come true if you
believe and strive for excellence. So never say "can't"!

Blessings,

Mary L. Wilson

Dedication

I dedicate this book to Lizzie Wilson, known as Big Mama to the Wilson family.Mary Lee Wilson, Rosie Lee Wilson, Virginia "Dump" Wilson, Rev. Bennie Wilson, Donald Ray Wilson, Charles Wilson and Roosevelt "Jabby" Wilson, your memories live on and on for eternity.

Lamar "Keke" Anderson, Milton "Pooh" Manning and Mark, we love and miss you all so much, and you will never be forgotten. I also dedicate this book to all my readers and to those who supported me along the way. All our people who are locked down—Big Dre, Aubrey Yates and Quentin Johnson—I'll see you when you hit the bricks.

One thing is for certain, and two are for sure: when you do positive things, you get positive results.

Chapter 1

In Da Hood

Riding down the streets of Arlington and Wabada, the west side of the Lou—St. Louis that is. Libra, Mya and Reesie were out, on a fall evening, looking for the budman. Mya spotted the banana muffin standing next to his old school Delta 88, wiping down his 22-inch rims.

"Damn! There he go wit' his sexy ass," stated Mya.

Libra looked in his direction and said, "You shole right! Sexy is what he is." Reesie was speechless as she stared.

Mya called the guy to the car. He's known as Keke in the street, but Lamar Larkins is the name his mother gave him at birth. As he approached the car, the ladies noticed his bowlegs. The ladies thought they were seeing a model off the GQ magazine. Once he was up close and personal, the guy was very handsome, or should I say fine as a muthafucka. He had a perfect set of teeth. They were white as snow, with two slugs at the bottom on each side of his mouth. His big beautiful eyes were chestnut brown with thick eyebrows and long eyelashes to accommodate them.

Keke wore a low haircut with subterranean waves. If you stared too long you became seasick. Standing at six feet one and with the tightest biceps, Mr. Larkins was well groomed at all times. He sported a blue Dickey outfit. His shirt was left open so his black wife-beater could show. Last but not least, he wore a pair of Chuck Taylor Converse tennis shoes. His mannerism was of a thug nigga, but that didn't take anything away from him because he was all so scrumptious to look at.

"What's crackin' Baby girl?" asked Keke.

"Try'na blow my brains out," uttered Mya.

"I got that head-banger boogie, that fire, that heat, that in doe. What cha want? I got it."

"Lemme get a dub," Mya said excitedly. After the transaction, Keke resumed pleasantries with Libra and Reesie.

"Aw yeah, Baby girl. There's a lil sumthin' extra 'cause ya'll always spent proper wit' a nigga. And Ladybug, when you gon' let a nigga take you out? You know, wine and dine you like a queen suppose to be, and even make you my Mrs."

"Good looking out, big bro," Mya said to Keke.

"Fo' sho'!" Keke responded with some of his favorite words. "I gotta look out for my peeps."

"Keke, my name is Libra—not Ladybug. And no, you can't wine and dine me and absolutely cannot make me your Mrs.!" Libra replied with an attitude.

"Why is that?" Keke asked aggressively.

"I don't think you're ready for me," Libra stated, rolling her eyes and twisting her neck.

"Oh yeah?" Keke replied, rubbing his chin.

"Oh yeah!" Libra responded nonchalantly.

"What brings you to that conclusion?"

"You did."

"How's that?"

"Look Keke, this ain't no twenty questions. Now let it go."

Keke loved the challenge and denial Libra put forth. It made his dick hard and he knew he had to have her.

"You know what Ladybug? I'll see you again; you know this a small world. You'll be dreamin' 'bout me sweetness. You gon' be lookin' for me in the day-time with a flashlight. Watch!"

"No! I don't think so sweetie, 'cause I don't dream and you're already a light bulb," stated Libra seductively.

2

The way Libra moved her lips made Keke's dick even harder. Every time he saw her, he tried to get at her. "Well. Baby girl, I'ma let you ladies disappear and ya come back real soon, ya hear?" Keke stated mocking the Beverly Hillbillies.

"Thank you again, Boo." Mya butted in.

"Aw yeah, Ladybug. You be good."

"Boo Boo, I'm always good, even when I'm bad."

"I know. I'm try'na see how good," Keke whispered as he walked away from the car.

Libra had to admit it. Keke was sexy as hell and she also wanted to know if he was as good as she'd heard he was. Throughout the conversation, Reesie remained silent.

Libra was a beautiful creature. She was very voluptuous, with a figure any woman would kill for. She stood about five feet five and had firm breasts that stood at attention with or without support. Her eyes were huge and they were cold black. She was versatile when it came to her hair, no matter how she wore it. Today it was in a long wrap with very short bangs in the front and streaks of auburn. She has a caramel complexion. Libra never applied any makeup to her skin. It was remarkably smooth. She always wore Mac lip-gloss to give a shine to her full lips. Her lips always seemed to draw a lot of attention, because of the way they were shaped. Everywhere she went, she was envied. She had the sweetest heart. Libra was every man's dream and every woman's nightmare.

Her friends nicknamed her Scales because her zodiac sign was Libra. But her most stunning assets were her deep dimples and her beauty marks, also known as sexy moles. The little black dots covered her entire body. They are considered a sign of sexiness, and sexy she was. She also had a slug in her mouth on one of her bottom left teeth.

The ladies rode to PRJ's liquor store on St. Louis Avenue and Union Boulevard to retrieve a box of White Owl blunts and a six-pack of Glaciers Bay Coolers and Busch beer.

When they arrived, Mya was running off at the mouth as usual. "Hoes, get ya'lls cheese together, 'cause my funds are runnin' short. Ya'll know I gotta get my, *Bitch U Spend Cash Here,* drink."

Reesie looked at Mya with her nose turned in the air like something stank and said, "Bitch, when you seen that nigga Keke, you would've thought you hit the lottery or sumthin'. We had our cheese together, and you said I got it! You see what a dick can do to you, bitch? We know you only got enough cheese for yo' Busch."

The ladies broke into a hysterical laugh.

Reesie and Mya exited the car to enter the store. As they walked away, Mya asked Libra, "Hey Ms. Stuck Up! Would you like anythin' else?"

Libra looked at Mya and rolled her eyes. With the middle finger up, and rolling it around, she said, "Bitch, go fuck yo'self."

Libra's mouth was lethal in more ways than one. While the ladies were in the store Libra sat in her black 2003 Chrysler 300 listening to Jill Scott singing, *Is It the Way?* Libra also had a beautiful voice and music was her first love.

All of a sudden Libra saw Reesie running to the car. Libra asked her, "What the fuck's wrong with you?"

"Where's the crow bar?"

"Why?"

"So I can bust those bitches' heads!"

Reesie was angry as hell walking to the back of the car. Libra asked no further questions and automatically popped the trunk.

Entering the small store, Libra grabbed one girl off Mya and slashed her face with her blade. She grabbed the girl by her hair and said, "Rat, raise up off her!" Once she was angry, there was no controlling her.

Reesie had one girl pinned against the ice machine and was beating the shit out of her with the crowbar. She told the girl, "Bitch, I gives no fuck about you. I gotta green card, so there. If the State thinks I'm crazy, I'ma act like it on you."

Mya did her demo on big girl. People were trying to contain the trio but couldn't. The owner of the store informed them that one time was on the way.

Reesie said, "So what! These hoes act up and they get smacked up."

Libra, not knowing who was holding her, felt a firm grip on her arm. She turned to her left and noticed it was Keke who was holding her arm. Knowing the recognizable smell of his cologne, she spoke calmly.

"Keke, please release me. You know you don't hold nobody when they're bangin'. I'm good!" Libra was annoyed as hell but remained composed.

"Are you sure?" Keke confirmed affectionately.

"Yes, positive," she answered.

There was something about this woman that made Keke's dick stand taller than the St. Louis Arch. And there was something about this man that made Libra's pussy wetter than the Mississippi River.

Knowing the cops was on the way, Keke ordered Gemini, "Man, get the ladies and get little. Take them to the honeycomb hideout and get at me when ya'll get situated. Rhonda will have everythin' together and waitin' for ya'll. Take care of her first."

Rhonda was Keke's best friend, and she had her shit together. She always looked out for him like a big sister. Rhonda left and went to Morris Brown College after they

5

graduated from high school but she came back to the Lou and has been by Keke's side ever since.

"In a minute," Gemini said to Keke. With that, he got the ladies and kept it movin'.

"Papa, I'll take care of the damages. Just give me the bill and I'll have someone come in and fix what needs to be done," Keke assured the owner of the store.

Papa didn't have a problem with that. "Sure will, nephew," he replied.

The other three females had to wait on the ambulance. They were fucked up pretty bad. When the cops arrived they questioned the bystanders, but no one said a word about what happened—not Papa or his workers. The three girls were then transported to Barnes Jewish Hospital.

Chapter 2

Chillin'

Gemini took the girls to the Airport Hilton Hotel. He made sure each girl had her own room, just as he was instructed. Gemini asked no questions because he knew Keke's m.o. After the ladies were settled, they all chilled in Libra's room. Gemini grabbed a room for himself and Keke also.

"Yo' Ma, ya'll need to chill here tonight."

"Yo' Poppy, why?" Mya asked in a Spanish accent.

"'Cuz ya'll know them broads done pressed charges. They were fucked up real bad."

"Them hoes shouldn't been trippin'. Mya, why were we bangin' with them broads anyway?" Libra inquired.

"Dig Scales, when Reesie and I walked in the store, those nasty bitches were blockin' the doorway. As I entered, I said 'excuse me' twice. That big bitch moved, but that hoe that looks like she got that package said 'yeah whateva'.' Before I knew it, Reesie jumped in the girl's face and asked her, 'Do you have a hitch wit' my sistah or me?' The skinny chick said, 'I don't know you or yo' sistah, and don't give a fuck 'bout ya'll hoes.' Reesie reached out and touched the bitch like AT&T, and she fell."

Reesie intervened in the conversation and said, "Big girl ran up and got knocked the fuck out wit' a can of Campbell soup, 'cause that's what her big ass be eatin', 'cause that mouth is on swoll!"

The ladies and Gemini laughed. Gemini was actually having a good time with them and also digging Mya.

"Reesie, why did you need a crow bar? You weren't playin' wit' that hoe, huh? " asked Libra.

"See, I want them hoes to think about that ass-kickin' they got. Next time them hoe's gon' feel that lead and think twice before they open their muthafuckin' mouths and fuck wit' my sistah."

"Girl, you ain't got no sistahs," confirmed Mya, teasingly.

"Well you better pretend like you my sistah, bitch!" Reesie said, laughing. Not feel good all of sudden, she up off the floor and walked to the bathroom. Gemini was tickled pink. Libra and Mya looked at him and busted out laughing themselves.

"Scales, you put in some work too. You sliced that girl's face like an onion," Mya said, imitating Libra as she spoke.

"Those hoes got out of line. They got dealt wit' plain and simple, na!" she said, turning her nose up like something stank as usual.

The girls did act like real sisters. They had each other's back no matter what, and they were strapped at all times. When Mya and Reesie first met Libra, they said she was stuck-up, but they knew she was down for her crown.

"Put that blunt in the air, Mya," Libra yelled to her. "Gemini, you wanna hit it?"

"Hell yeah, Ma!"

After the blunt was gone, Gemini excused himself and went to his room.

"Scales, check this out. Ol' girl whose face you cut, she looked very familiar."

"Yeah I know, but I can't put a finger on it."

Coming from the bathroom, Reesie interjected, "I was thinkin' the same thing to myself. It'll come to me eventually. That bitch looks like she's a static hoe."

8

"I'm hip," Mya said slowly, high from the hydro she smoked.

"Ya'll, we need to know what's really good wit' them hoes, 'cause if they trip, it's like that for them. Think that's a lie? That's what the fuck is up," Libra said as she moved her hand, trying to make them understand it's whatever and she means that.

"Scales, you hip as a muthafucka'."

"Mya, ya'll don't know nothin' 'bout me fo' real, lil baby."

"Girl, what the fuck eva'. But what I do know is you feelin' yo'self when you should be lettin' that sexy ass nigga Keke feel you," Mya said as she danced around the room.

"I'm not afraid to touch myself. Ya'll heard what T-Boz said," Libra said, moving her hips like a hula-hoop, rubbing her hands over her body and singing the song seductively.

Mya and Reesie looked at each other and said. "That's my dog!"

The ladies laughed and gave each other hi fives.

"A'ight, a'ight," Libra said holding her stomach from laughing so hard. "Ya'll gotta go." She walked to the door and opened it and said. "Good day, ladies."

Reesie and Mya follow behind her saying, "This freaks puttin' us out for real."

"Love ya'll," Libra said as she closed the door.

Libra had just disrobed when she heard a knock at the door. She walked to the door in her Polo sports bra and Polo boy shorts. Libra did not look out the peephole. She knew it was one of her friends, if not both of them. She opened the door and Keke was standing there with one yellow rose in his hand. Libra didn't know what to do or say, so she stood there and held Keke's stare.

He examined her body from head to toe and said, "Damn! If this is heaven, I made it! Thank ya Lord, thank ya."

Libra cracked a half smile and said, "Boy, that's one person you don't play wit'."

"Who said I'm playin'? Maybe I'm givin' thanks for his many blessings. We all have our own personal relationship with God. I know I do, Ladybug."

"Can I come in?" Keke asked as he walked in.

Libra did not respond to his request. She stepped to the side as he entered the hotel room. As he walked pass her, she was mesmerized by the smell of his Truth cologne by Calvin Klein. His bowlegs made him look like he's ridden a horse his whole life. Once he reached the living room area, he noticed candles burning and music playing. "What you know about The Isley Brothers?"

"Same as you, evidently," Libra said, closing the door and not realizing she had that much skin revealed. This man had her wide open.

"Would you excuse me a sec, Keke?" Libra rushed into the other room.

"Don't rush on my account," thought Keke, devilishly.

"Boy, you're sumthin' else."

"Yeah, I know. I'm beginning to believe that myself. That's what they tell me."

"You're a little conceited, huh?"

"Naw, Princess. Just one hundred percent real, ya know!" Keke confidently stated.

"Oh yeah."

"Fo'sho'." Keke said, kissing Libra on her left cheek where her dimple was.

"Keke, thank you for the rose."

"No! Thank you for the new friendship that's about to jump off."

"Who said we were friends?"

"You did."

"No, I didn't," Libra said with a bamboozled look on her face.

"Beautiful! Beautiful!"

Keke grabbed Libra by her arms and pulled her close to him. "Babe when you accepted the rose you said yes."

Looking into his enormous eyes, Libra's pussy became moist..

"I did accept the rose, didn't I?"

"Yes, you did Ladybug. The yellow rose does mean friendship."

"I can be yo' friend. Nothin' beats a try," Libra stated throwing her hands in the air.

"You shole right Ladybug. Now, can we shake to a new friendship?"

"Fo sho!" Libra said, imitating Keke.

He fractured a smile. "Dig Lil Mama. I'm so serious about this friendship. I need a woman like you on my team." Keke was holding the bottom of Libra's chin. "Call my room 269 in the mornin' when you wake up so we can do breakfast," he said, pulling Libra to him and kissing the tip of her nose.

As he turned to leave, Libra grabbed his arm lightly and pulled him to her. She stood on her tiptoes and kissed his forehead. Keke exited the hotel room and kept it movin'.

This has been a crazy day, but also a lovely day, Libra thought.

Ring, ring! Libra was awakened by the telephone.

"Hello," Libra said, still semi-asleep.

"Good mornin', Ladybug."

"Good mornin' yo'self, Keke."

"What's crackin?"

"My stomach," Libra muttered while stretching and yawning.

"That's why I called. How long will it take you to get dressed?"

"About thirty minutes."

"See you in thirty minutes, beautiful."

"Uh huh," Libra said as she disconnected the call.

Ring, ring! The phone rang again.

"Yeah!" Libra barked after removing the phone from its cradle.

"Scales, my stomach touchin' my back."

"Damn Mya girl, you're real hungry," Libra said, getting out of bed.

"Damn right. Are you dressed?"

"Almost," Libra lied.

"We'll be in the VIP area of the dining room."

"Uh huh," Libra replied as she disconnected the second call.

On her way out the door Libra checked herself once more in the mirror. She admired her Apple bottom jeans. She had on a very low-cut shirt, showing her tattoo above her right breast that read LIBRA in Chinese. She wore jeans that hugged her hips like a second layer of skin. You could see the outline of her Victoria Secret thongs. She also had a tattoo on her lower back of a scale with two cherries on one side making the scale unbalanced. It read GOOD DAYZ on the side that was up and BAD DAYZ on the side that was down.

She also had on a fresh pair of Air Max tennis shoes. When she entered the dining area, everyone was already seated. The table setup was splendid. Gemini, Mya and Reesie sat on one side. Libra and Keke shared the other side. Keke greeted Libra with a kiss on the tip of her nose and a yellow rose and made sure she was seated. Libra was a breath of fresh air to Keke. She was so gorgeous to him. From the way her lips moved when words came out of her mouth to the way her hips swayed from side to side when she walked. He thought she was the sexiest woman breathing.

Breakfast turned out to be beautiful. The ladies gave Keke the details about the incident from the day before. Everyone decided to chill out for the remainder of the day. No one had really got any rest the night before. Keke and Libra unwound and talked for the remainder of the day. She did not know what to think about this state of affairs with Keke, but one thing she did know was she liked him. He charmed the shit out of her.

They lay in bed, watching *Love and Basketball* and *Love Jones*, both Libra's favorite movies. Libra hit pause on the movie.

"Keke, I have a question I wanna ask you."

"Speak, babe. Ask me anythin' you wanna know."

"What is it that you want from me or wit' me, for that matter?"

"You, baby."

"No, all jokes aside." Libra stated seriously.

"Who said I'm joking?"

"I'm just sayin', we've known each other for years and ..." Libra stopped in the middle of her sentence.

"And what, Libra? I've been at you for years, but you always played a nigga to the left."

"We've exchanged numbers on several occasions." Libra looked Keke directly in the eyes.

"What's wrong, beautiful?"

"I can never recollect a time when I heard you call me Libra. It's always been Ladybug or whateva' you

13

decided to call me that was fascinating or charming. You know how you do it, Mr. Larkins."

"Well, get use to it, Mrs. Larkins."

Intrigued by his last comment, Libra picked up the phone to check on her friends-sisters. No answer in Mya's room so she tried Reesie's room.

Ring, ring! "Hello." Reesie answered the phone in a sleepy nature.

"Did I wake you?" asked Libra.

"No, not really," Reesie said yawning. "What's good?"

"Just seein' what you were doin'."

"Chillin', gettin' ready to fire up," Reesie said as she yawned again.

"Do you know where that freak is?"

"I think she's in ol' boy's room."

"Gemini!" Libra stated, surprised.

"Yeah, Gemini," bitched Reesie sarcastically.

"Damn Res, what's wrong?" Libra asked compassionately. "You musta talked to Caelin?"

"Yeah, not too long ago. Scales, I'm sorry. I didn't mean to crack on you."

"So what ya'll gon' do? Try and work it out?" Libra asked trying to lighten up the mood.

"Yeah, he says we are. We're goin' to get together tomorrow and talk, because he says he misses me, and I miss him so much, Scales. I promise I do," Reesie said, venting.

"Whateva' you decide to do, I'm here for you. We're in this together derrty. I know you've been a little preoccupied lately," Libra told Reesie, sounding so sincere

"I do have a lot on my mind these days, Scales."

"Call me if you need to talk or want me to come to yo' room, okay Boo? You know you my sistah, girl," Libra

14

Ghetto Luv

said, releasing much love to Reesie. "You know I love you."

"Off top, but I don't wanna take you from that sexy ass man you wit'."

"I got this. This is on lock. Please believe me," Libra said as they laughed and disconnected the call.

"Is everything okay, baby?" Keke asked as he reached for Libra to lie down.

"Yes everything's superior."

"I know, and time will prove me right."

"Oh yeah," whispered Libra flirtatiously.

"Fo' sho', Lil Mama!" The chemistry between Keke and Libra was unbelievable. Libra leaned over and kissed Keke on his forehead.

"Lil Mama, what's up wit' that?"

"You." Libra pointed to him.

Keke climbed on top of Libra and caressed her entire body. As he kissed her, he whispered sweet things in her ear. "Ladybug I want you all to myself," he said as he kissed her eyes. "I want you in my life. No, I need you in my life," he whispered as he kissed her neck. "You'll never want or need fo' anythin'."

Libra grabbed Keke's face with both hands and looked closely into his day dreamy eyes and said, "Who said I wanted or needed for anythin'? Please make me know it. Babe, you know this the show-me state."

"Fo' sho," Keke said, trying to gain his composure. But the sight of Libra would not allow that to happen. He started kissing her passionately, and things quickly got out of control. Libra panicked a bit and lifted Keke off her.

"Baby, I'm hungry."

"Me too, but not fo' food. Fo' you!" Keke said, sucking his teeth.

15

"Boy, let's order room service," Libra said. She kissed Keke on the forehead and picked up the phone to order room service.

"Whateva' yo' lil heart desires, Ladybug."

Chapter 3

Break Up to Make Up

Reesie hoped Caelin was at the house, because her patience was running thin with him. But to her surprise, when she turned the corner of their street and pulled into the four-car garage, she saw his black F150 Rams truck and his gold SS Monte Carlo parked in his assigned area, which read: Lay Lay. Reesie parked her burned orange Rodeo truck in her assigned area, which read: Re Re. It was the only space available, because her 1986 white Cutlass Supreme was in its rightful place. Caelin never ceased to amaze her.

When Reesie pulled into the garage, she noticed it looked different. Caelin had had their names repainted with the labels of their cars on it, too.

Muthafucka' knows how to make up when he does sumthin' wrong, Reesie thought.

Entering the living room from the garage, Reesie heard one of her favorite songs playing: "Love of My Life," by Erykah Badu and Common. Caelin knew he was the love of Reesie's life. Their relationship had been unsteady for quite some time, but overall, Reesie knew Caelin loved and adored her as much as she loved and adored him. He was dreadfully short-tempered at times, and he did things he regretted later.

When Reesie entered the house, an abnormal feeling came upon her, as if someone else been present in her home. As Caelin approached her, he could see that something was bothering her, and he asked, "Res, what's wrong?"

"Nothin', just a little thrown-off, like Mystikal. That's all," Reesie stated smartly.

"Well let me handle that, baby, okay?" stated Caelin sincerely.

"Make me know it then," Reesie said as she walked past Caelin and entered the kitchen. Caelin followed behind her like a puppy dog.

"Boo, you hungry?"

"Yes. What you got?" Reesie asked with her hands on her hips.

"Yo' favorite," he said, grabbing her hand and walking to the table. Before he pulled her chair out to seat her, Caelin gave her a little black box. "Baby, open it right now."

Reesie opened the box and found a Winnie the Pooh pendant inside. Reesie loved Winnie the Pooh.

"Thank you, Lay Lay, but if you buy me any more Winnie the Pooh stuff, I won't have anywhere to put it."

"We'll make room, baby. Now, eat yo' food befo' it gets cold. You know it don't taste the same in the microwave, and I don't feel like cookin' again," Caelin said, smiling.

"Boy! Yeah right. What you mean to say is that you don't wanna drive back to the city to Goody Goody Diner." Goody Goody was a diner on Natural Bridge Boulevard that served the best breakfast in town. "I do love how you set the table wit' the Winnie the Pooh placemats and tablecloth. This is pretty. You act like you slaved over the stove all mornin'. Thank you, baby, for everythin', but I'm still pissed at you."

After breakfast, Reesie walked into the living room while Caelin cleaned the kitchen. Reesie still had this troubled feeling that she couldn't shake.

"Caelin!" Reesie called. "Caelin!" she called again.

"Yeah boo," Caelin answered, walking into the living room.

"Did you stay here last night?"

"Yeah. Why ya ask me that?"

"I know you didn't clean the house this mornin'. You had to have started last night. You dusted and vacuumed the whole nine.

"After talkin' to ya last night, I wanted everythin' to be perfect. Now that you're here, the only thin' ya gotta do is relax."

"I appreciate that, Lay Lay." Reesie kissed Caelin on the lips and he walked back in the kitchen.

Sitting down on the couch, Reesie realized how much she missed her home. They had an extravagant home. Everything was white and gold. The furniture was white trimmed with gold. The carpet was very plush, and there was a real mink lion head in the center of the floor. The coffee and end tables was lion heads also. The lion heads held the glass to the tables. The ceiling fans were very high and were controlled with remote controls, which were also white and gold. Reesie looked on the wall to her left and admired the picture of her and Caelin. Libra had taken it at Caelin's birthday party last year. Libra had the portrait enlarged to make a giant poster. She had given it to Reesie as a housewarming gift.

Reesie walked to the stereo to change the CD. Her stereo system had a three hundred-disc changer. She removed the remote control from its cradle and found what she was looking for. R. Kelly's "12 Play."

"Baby come over here and have a seat," Caelin said, pulling her by her hand and walking her to the couch. Once they were seated Reesie turned to face Caelin and said.

"Lay Lay, this arguin' and fightin' shit is gettin' real old and played out. Baby look, either we get it together or we go our separate ways. Caelin I love you, I promise to

God I do, but I love me more. I will not continue to let you put your hands on me and treat me like I'm a nigga on the streets. You dog walk me. I will not walk around here mad at the world when I'm only mad at you. I will not leave my house again. You will leave next time. You know what Caelin? There won't be a next time. Boo, you my man," Reesie said with tears rolling down her face. "You suppose to make me happy and vice versa."

"Boo, I don't make ya happy?" asked Caelin honestly.

"Of course you do, when we're not fightin'. I love the things you do for me, the places you take me, and I'm even more intrigued by the nice gifts you buy me. My happiness is much more important to me than all that materialistic shit. Look Caelin, you're my everythin', but I'd rather be unhappy than to be wit' you and be miserable. I mean that, Boo, and the next time you put yo' hands on me I will kill you! If I don't kill you, you gonna wish you were dead. I'm gonna fuck you up real bad." Reesie looked Caelin straight in his eyes and asked him. "Do I make myself clear?"

"Baby, every day ain't gonna be peaches and cream," avowed Caelin caringly.

"Again, do I make myself clear, Caelin?" Reesie asked again, speaking the words very slowly.

"Yeah, stink."

" And another thing Lay Lay. I will not deal wit' them other bitches either."

"Baby ya won't have to deal with none of that bullshit no mo', 'cuz it won't happen. Res, I promise I will never eva' put my hands on ya again. Just the thought of ya leavin' me drives me the fuck crazy. Girl, I love ya. I love ya mo' than life itself. Boo, I'ma do whateva' I have to do to prove that to ya or die tryin'. Res ya are my future, and without ya, I'm shitless. I love ya so much. Girl, ya gon' be

20

the mother of my seed one day," declared Caelin affectionately.

"Caelin, baby, I love you, too, and you're my future as well, but we need another solution. Listen, I'm willin' to try once more if you are."

"That's all gravy, baby," responded Caelin.

"It better be," Reesie said, smiling at her man.

"Baby, can we make up now? Ya know—break up to make up."

"Boy, you just want some of this neck."

"Res, like Biggie said, if ya don't know, now ya know, ya know."

Reesie loved this man with all her heart and soul, and her mission was to please him by any means necessary.

She looked at her man seductively and said in a very low voice, almost a whisper, "Stand up."

Caelin did what he was told and stood up. Reesie unbuttoned and unzipped his pants, and they fell to the floor. Caelin stepped out of them. Reesie pushed Caelin down on the couch and removed all of her clothes except for the black lace Prada underwear and the hot pink stiletto shoes. He watched as she danced to R. Kelly's "Bump and Grind." Reesie kissed her man from head to toe, but when she reached his manhood all her attention focused on it. She grabbed his dick and deep throated it like it was the last lollypop on earth. When Caelin couldn't take it anymore, he removed her head and lifted her to her feet. "Ms. Wright, turn around and drop it like it's hot."

Reesie fulfilled his request. She knew that turned Caelin on. Reesie bent over and touched her toes, spreading her legs. She knew what was about to go down. Before Caelin resumed pleasing Reesie's body, he admired her body. Reesie was thick—as Caelin would say, "Monkey thick."

Caelin got down on his knees, opened Reesie lips from behind and sucked all her love juice. Reesie loved the way this man made her feel. Reesie got on top of Caelin and rode him like a cowgirl. She slowly grinded on his dick, asking him while looking him in his eyes, "You miss this pussy, don't cha?"

"Yes, Ms. Wright," said a hypnotized Caelin as he grabbed her bodacious hips with the handlebar tattoos on each side.

Reesie rode Caelin like never before. After about forty-five minutes of erotic love making, their bodies erupted in ecstasy. They lay there and talked for a while, cuddled up together, loving each other's company. Then they drifted off to sleep.

Ring, ring! Reesie was awakened by the telephone.

"Hello," she said sleepily.

"Did I wake you?" asked Libra.

"No."

"Are you alright? You've been sleepin' a lot lately."

"I'm a little tired, Scales, that's all."

"I called to let you know that them hoes outta the hospital."

Reesie broke her embrace from Caelin and removed herself from the living room to the kitchen.

"Straight! How you know? It don't matter how you know, Scales, 'cause if they trip again, they gon' be back in the muthafuckin' hospital."

"Yeah, that's my point exactly, Res."

"You talk to Mya?"

"Yeah. That freak's with Gemini. She called a minute ago to invite us to a comedy show tonight at Club 314."

"Scales, I'm down."

"Reesie, meet us at the mall."

"What mall, bitch?"

"Northwest Plaza, girl."

"Bitch, that ol' ghetto ass mall?" confirmed Reesie.

"Yeah, that ol' ghetto fabulous ass mall, hoe. Where you wanna go? To the Galleria?"

"Fo' sho'!" Reesie said, imitating Keke and laughing.

"Reesie, you're real cute," Libra snapped, looking at the phone and rolling her eyes. "If we don't find anythin' at Ghetto Northwest Plaza, we'll go to the Galleria. I wanna eat at the Cheese Cake factory, anyway."

"Girl, yo' ass is greedy. I knew it was a catch. Lemme jump in the shower and get a couple of grand from Lay, and I'm there," Reesie whispered.

"Yeah, wash that ass, 'cause Lay Lay's been puttin' miles on it, and it's time for an oil change," Libra confirmed, amused.

"Scales, you got jokes and I'm out."

"Good day," Libra said and with that they disconnected the call and kept it movin'.

Chapter 4

What's Done in the Dark Will Come to Light

Libra and Mya jumped into the 300. Mya pulled out a blunt and fired it up. They were listening to Hip-Hop station 100.3, The Beat. They were jamming all Tupac's songs because it was the anniversary of his death. They were playing, *Can You Get Away?* That was Libra's jam. She rapped along with the song.

> *Could it be my destiny, to be lonely?*
> *Checkin' for dem hoochies that be on me 'cuz*
> *they phony.*
> *With chew it different.*
> *I got no need to be suspicious.*
> *'Cuz I can tell.*
> *My life with you would be delicious.*
> *The way ya lick ya lips and shake ya hips got*
> *me addicted.*

"Damn, Scales! Who you got on yo' mind when you sing that song?" Mya said looking at her friend, thunderstruck.

"See, first of all, the line of buz'ness is to mind yo' buz'ness. That's just one of my favorite verses in that rap. Why you all up in mines anyway? Do sumthin' constructive and call Res and see where she's at, bitch."

Mya called Reesie on her cell phone, but not before rolling her eyes at Libra and saying, "Whateva', rat." They laughed.

Ring, ring!

"Res where are you?"

"I'm pullin' up now."

"Meet us in Famous Barr. You know the spot."

"Okay," Reesie said and hung up.

"Scales, Reesie been actin' real strange these days."

"Yeah, I know. When I talked to her this mornin', I asked her was she okay, and she said she's just tired."

"I hope that's what it is, because if it's that puck ass nigga Caelin, he gon' come up missin', and the trash man gon' find his body stankin' if he put his hands on her and I know 'bout it."

"I feel you, ghetto girl," Libra said to Mya, smiling.

The girls had been friends since the third grade, and they were loyal to each other. Libra and Mya saw Reesie, as they got closer to the women's session. Reesie walked up to them and they all hugged.

"What's up, Res? What's poppin'?" Mya asked Reesie.

"Not too much of nothin' but that damn gum I'ma 'bout to take out of Scales' mouth."

Libra found the perfect outfit. She purchased a DKNY army fatigue set. The pants were hip huggers. As usual, her shirt showed a lot of cleavage. Reesie bought a blue denim Rocawear dress, and Mya purchased an off-white Baby Phat cat suit

The ladies strolled down to the shoes department. Libra found the nastiest fatigue Timberlands stiletto boots, along with the matching purse and hat. Mya got off-white stiletto shoes and a matching purse. Reesie bought some blue denim stilettos and purse.

"I still wanna go to the Galleria," Reesie said.

"That's cool. I wanna eat at the Cheese Cake Factory and get me some sexy undies from Lord and Taylor," said Libra.

"It's the freak in you, bitch," Mya said to Libra.

"Yes sir. Yes sir!" stated Libra with a Midwest accent.

While leaving the mall, the ladies were spotted by Nutcase and Slick, the two most dangerous niggas in the Lou. Nutcase had spent five years in prison for killing his girlfriend's family, including his girlfriend and his two kids. Slick would talk his way out of any situation and was fine as hell. He'd kill a nigga on sight.

"What's good?" Nutcase asked the ladies.

"Shit," said Mya the first one to speak.

"Not too much of nothin', slow motion," replied Libra.

"Chillin'," confirmed Reesie.

"Peep game," said Slick. "Ol' girl and dem been askin' 'bout ya'll. Yeah, Baby girl, she asked Jokah the other day. Ya know Jokah wanted a wet one, and as always, he volunteered info. I told him to tell dem hoes to stay in the lil league, 'cuz ya'll pack that steel," Slick said to Mya, wishing he could bake that thang. "Fuck the shit out of her."

"Libra, ya'll ladies too fine to be fighting."

"Nutcase, you're right about that. That's why I pack that thang. I ain't got time to be playin' wit' these ol' silly ass girls."

"It's whateva', Slick. Tell Jokah get at me. Here's my cell number."

"A'ight, Baby girl, will do."

"I wish they would come trippin'. I got sumthin' for that ass," Reesie bitched.

"Hey Libra, let me holla at you for a second." Nutcase excused himself and Libra obliged his request.

"Pretty, I would like it so much if you would accompany me to dinner and a movie real soon."

Libra was surprised and caught completely off guard. He caught her with her mouth open.

"Baby, close your mouth."

"Damn, Nutcase, my fault. Shit just been crazy lately. I'm surprised that's all, but to answer yo' question, no, I don't think so."

"Well, if you ever change your mind, here's my card." Nutcase reached into his Sean John blazer jacket. "Give me a call anytime."

Libra accepted the card.

"A'ight, Nutcase," said Libra delicately.

"No, call me Tyron."

"Sure, Tyron," Libra repeated, and they joined the others.

"Slick, good lookin' out, man," Mya stated with appreciation.

"Aw' yeah, Baby girl. Nigga got yo' back and front, too," he said in a very serious tone, and with that they departed.

After getting this information from Nutcase and Slick, the girls decided against going to the Galleria. They stood on the parking lot of the mall, trying to decide what to do next, "I'm hungry. Let's go to the Royal Palace. We can eat and have a drink. It's happy hour, two for one," Libra suggested.

"Yeah, that's cool. We can drop my car off at home and I can get dressed at ya'll house tonight," declared Reesie.

"That's a done detta then," Mya said eagerly.

"Reesie parked her car in the garage and went into the house to retrieve her things. She exited the house carrying two Coach duffle bags, one brown and the other one black. Libra had already opened the trunk. Libra and Mya looked at each other, wondering why she had two bags. Mya, being as nosy as she was, asked, "Res, why do you have two bags?"

"Cause one is for my clothes and the other is for my shoes. You hoes don't believe in bringin' a bitch back home, so I need my spare, just like these ol'poot butt ass niggas," Reesie agitatedly bitched.

On the way to the RP, Mya called Gemini and Keke so they could meet them there.

"I'm not stepping on nobody toes, am I?" Mya asked, looking at Libra.

"It's good," Libra said to Mya, rolling her eyes.

"Bitch, we know its good. You want that nigga so bad you can taste that dick," stated Reesie.

"You don't know!" Libra said, rubbing her tongue across her top lip.

"When they arrived, they saw Keke's car. Libra looked in the mirror to check her appearance. She applied her Oh Baby lip-gloss that she'd purchased from the Mac. Mya and Reesie did the same.

Entering the club, the DJ was jamming. Libra sang along with Mary J. Blige, *I'm going down.* Keke, Gemini, Lorenzo and Ton-Loc had occupied a table with a bottle of Moet on chill. Keke immediately got a wood when he saw Libra. They made their way to the table and everyone exchanged pleasantries. Keke pulled the chair out for Libra to sit next to him. Mya and Reesie sat next to Gemini. Lorenzo got the waitress's attention, and she came to the table to take their orders.

"Good evening, ladies. My name is Tonya, and I'll be ya'll's waitress this evening. How can I help you?"

"Where's Bunkie? Is she not workin' this evening?" Mya inquired.

"Yes she is. Would you like for me to send her over?"

"Yes please." Mya said. "I don't mean any harm."

"None taken," said Tonya maliciously.

"I know that bitch ain't try'na get smart," Reesie bitched. "I'll beat the shit outta her."

"Chill Res, we got enough static now," stated Libra. Bunkie walked to the table and embraced the ladies.

"Ya'll want the usual right?"

"Yeah and we wanna order sumthin' to eat also."

"I knew that also, Mya. You didn't have to tell me that."

"Fellas, can I get ya'll anythin' else?"

"Fo' sho'," said Keke. "Give me a Grey Goose and Cranberry juice, Remy on the rocks and Martell straight and a Witches Brew."

After Bunkie took their orders she went to retrieve them.

"Ladybug, you look lovely as usual." Keke complimented Libra on how attractive she looked.

"Thank you sir, you don't look half bad yo'self," Libra said to Keke, returning the compliment. Lee, the rose man entered the club, and Keke excused himself from the table. He met the rose man and asked him to take three roses to his table. He wanted Libra to have the rose with the red teddy bear attached and a single rose for Mya and Reesie.

Bunkie and Keke came back to the table at the same time. Bunkie gave the women their drinks first.

"Libra, here's your Grey Goose and Cranberry. Mya, here's your Seagram's Gin and a splash of orange juice, and Res, yo' Remy Red."

Bunkie then sat the fellows' drinks in front of them. . Once Keke was settled, Libra gently grabbed his waist and kissed him on the lips.

"Thank you sexy for the rose and teddy bear." Caught off guard, Keke responded promptly.

"Fo' sho'. A beautiful rose and teddy bear for a beautiful lady." Keke stared Libra directly in those gigantic eyes of hers.

"Cut that shit out," Ton-Loc said playfully.

"Get a room," stated Mya, and everybody laughed. The DJ played Dru Hill, *The Love We Share Stays on My Mind.*

"Hey, that's my jam," shouted Libra, rocking side to side with her arms in the air, popping her fingers with her eyes closed.

"Ladybug, can I have this dance?"

"Yes you may," Libra said, showing her deep dimples.

Libra got up from her seat. Keke held his hand out and Libra folded hers into it as he led her to the dance floor.

Once they reached the dance floor, Libra put her arms around Keke's neck, and he grabbed her by her waist. They swayed from side to side. The Kenneth Cole cologne Keke wore intoxicated Libra. She closed her eyes as she sang the song in his ear. He was more captivated by her voice. His manhood was at full erection and she could feel the hardness against her. They drifted off into their own little world. Keke didn't notice Pooh standing next to them.

"This is why you don't have time for me no more? I knew it was another bitch. This same bitch that left this muthafuckin' scar on my face," said the deranged Pooh, with her finger pointed in Keke face.

"If you call me another bitch, this gon' be the same bitch that put some lead in that ass," Libra said.

"Look Pooh! Gon' wit' that shit. I already told you what's goin' down wit' us."

"Well why did you fuck me yesterday? Ol' nothin' ass nigga!"

"Cuz you let me. Now, burn out," Keke said, brushing her off with his hand.

30

Pooh wasn't leaving without static. She pushed Keke away from Libra. Keke grabbed Pooh by the neck.

"Ladybug, I'ma get at you later." Not waiting for a reply, he escorted Pooh out of the club.

Libra left the dance floor and walked to the bathroom. Reesie and Mya were leaving as she entered and they could tell something was wrong.

"Scales, what's wrong wit' you?" questioned Reesie.

"Ya'll know the bitch I engraved across the face at the liquor store?"

"Um huh," the ladies said in unison.

"Well, that's Keke bitch. She fronted him a minute ago. They should still be outside. He's probably whippin' that ass," said Libra, more hurt than mad.

"I couldn't put a finger on it then, but now I remember. I saw them at the St. Louis Mill Mall a couple of months ago when Jabby and I was together," stated Mya. "I was high as a muthafucka' too."

"It was meant for me to be in the bathroom, cause it woulda been on and poppin', and Keke woulda been payin' Big Joe for the damages in this muthafucka'," Reesie stated, displeased. "That's the bitch that jumped on that girl at the mall—her and about three other girls. The police was lookin' for them. The girl was in ICU."

"That's why I don't be fuckin' wit' these ol' fake ass niggas. They can't keep it real. If he had a woman, that's all he had to say." Libra was using her hands to talk, mad as hell. "I don't like it when people make decisions for me, and that's what he did by not tellin' me he had a woman. You ain't gotta lie to kick it, Craig," Libra fussed.

"Let's finish our drinks and blow this joint," Mya said.

The ladies walked back to the table, and Gemini, Lorenzo and Ton-Loc were still there.

"Ladybug, you good?"

"I'm so okay, Lorenzo. Thank you for askin', Boo."

The DJ continued to play good music. He played The Electric Slide, and they all went to the dance floor. For a minute Libra forgot about the incident with Keke. She loved being in his arms the short time she was allowed.

Chapter 5

What Goes Around Comes Around!

Libra asked Reesie to drive them to her house. She wanted to roll a blunt and make a call. Libra changed the CD player and played *It's all About Me* by Mya. Libra reclined her seat and removed the card with Nutcase's number. She usually star 67ed the number, but she dialed this number straight, without blocking.

Ring, ring!

"Yeah!" Nutcase said, sounding like he didn't want to be bothered.

"Did I catch you at a bad time? If so I can call back later."

"Nah, Pretty. I'm straight. What can I do for you?" Nutcase said in the sexiest voice Libra had ever witnessed.

"Well, Darkness, I called to arrange our date. You did give me that option, am I correct?" Libra stated very presumptuously.

"I didn't expect to hear from you so soon after the rejection you imposed on me."

"Tyron, I'm very unpredictable," Libra stated, passing the blunt to Mya and smiling.

"Baby love, you name the place and time. I'm there like clockwork," said Nutcase excitedly.

"What about tomorrow after five? The plannin' is up to you. I'll call you tomorrow and confirm the place and time. I'm on my way to a comedy show at Club 314," said Libra, revealing her whereabouts and thinking she knew Nutcase's next remark.

"Club 314? That's off the Rock Road."

33

"Um huh, yes it is," Libra said, rolling her neck with a smile on her face.

"My man, Lil Sam, is hosting the show. I'm also on my way there. So what's up wit' it? Can I be your date tonight, Pretty?" Nutcase grabbed his manhood as he asked. The thought of her gave him a hard-on.

"I don't see why not. I got my girls wit' me. Would that be a problem?"

"Boo, that's cool. Please be prompt. Nine o'clock. A'ight."

"Yes sir, daddy," Libra turned her lips up, thinking, *This nigga's aggressive, and I'm lovin' it.*

Libra, Reesie and Mya arrived at nine-o-five. The ladies made a grand entrance—well, the fellows thought so. Reesie walked in flossing her blue denim Rocawear mini dress with her blue denim stilettos with Rocawear written on the ass of the dress. Reesie wore a short hairdo with spikes all over.

Following behind Reesie was Mya, who sported a Baby Phat cat suit. She had off-white stilettos with a little pink in them, with the Baby Phat purse that was also off-white and pink. She wore a sixteen-inch Mohawk ponytail with a pink rose on the side of her head. The sixteen-inch ponytail could knock your eyes out if you got close enough.

Libra entered rocking a DKNY fatigue outfit. Her shirt was green, beige and black. The shirt is very low cut. It fitted like a second layer of skin. She had one pocket in the back and her name was imprinted on it. She wore her hair in a wrap with her fatigue hat cocked to the side, sporting her DKNY glasses.

Mya saw Gemini in the VIP session. The ladies approached the table. Gemini, Lorenzo and Ton-Loc were there. Ton-Loc had his girlfriend Tiffany with him. They had two kids and had lived together for four years. The ladies joined them, and Ton-Loc introduced them to

Tiffany. Lorenzo glorified the ladies on how gorgeous they looked. Gemini poured them a glass of Moet.

Libra wondered if Keke would be there or if he was with Pooh. She quickly discarded the thought. Looking at the back bar, she observed Nutcase conversing with an attractive female. That didn't bother Libra at all. She knew she was the shit. Libra excused herself from the others.

Libra walked over to Nutcase. Upon her arrival the female was leaving. As they passed one another, the woman rolled her eyes at Libra and Libra just smiled. "I thought you stood me up sweetheart," Nutcase said and kissed her on the cheek.

"No. I was runnin' behind. Were you tryin' to find a replacement?"

"No, never that baby," Nutcase said as he escorted her to his table, which wasn't far from Gemini's table.

"Tyron, you know if you tried to find a replacement, I would then be unattainable," Libra said, smiling. Nutcase had no problem getting a date, but Libra had a confident appearance about her that caught his undivided attention.

She is sexy as fuck, Nutcase thought to himself as Libra walked beside him. Of course Nutcase was on the outside, being the gentlemen that he was.

Nutcase stopped and spoke to Mya and Reesie. Lorenzo looked at Nutcase and said. "Derrty, I see yo' date finally arrived."

"Yeah, I thought I was stood up," Nutcase said, looking at Libra. That's what she'd wanted him to think. No man would have control over her. "I'll get at you later, fam." Nutcase gave all the men dap and kept it movin'.

Lil Sam came on stage to hype up the crowd. He told a few jokes, getting them ready for the first act. He then introduced St. Louis Slim. The crowd was stimulated. When St. Louis Slim came on stage, he looked around and said, "Fellas we have some sexy ass women in the Lou. If you don't know them, look around 'cuz ya'll asses must be blind. Even Stevie Wonder could see that. I saw this fine ass sistah up in here tonight. She wanna go to war, 'cuz she got on her gear. I swear fo' Lord I will be her prey. I surrender. Come and get me girl!" The crowd was elated with laughter.

St. Louis Slim continued to tell his jokes. Libra excused herself to the restroom. Mya and Reesie followed as she passed their table. Walking to the back of the club, someone grabbed Libra. She didn't know who it was, because the club was crowded. As she turned to see who it was, he was in her face.

"Ladybug, you are one beautiful creature," Keke said, fascinated by her DKNY perfume.

"Yeah, I've heard," Libra said as she turned to walk away, rolling her eyes.

"Baby, wait! I can explain everythin'. Look Ladybug, please believe none of what you see and half of what you hear."

"Keke, I'm here with someone else, and I don't want to be disrespectful. I keeps it real unlike some people. Good day." And with that Libra kept it movin'.

Keke followed behind her but lost her because she pushed her way through the crowd. He waited until she came out of the restroom. "Ladybug, I know you here with that nigga Nutcase. So what! What that mean to me?" Keke bitched, holding Libra hand.

"Where yo' bitch at? The one you fucked yesterday. Remember! Boy gon' wit' that bullshit. Keke go play games wit' somebody else, 'cause I'm not the one. Good day."

Libra kept it movin' on Keke ass. Libra left Mya and Reesie also.

"Fuck you, girl," Keke said as Libra walked away. "I'm not gonna kiss yo' ass," Keke bitched. His feelings were hurt, and he was not used to rejection.

"Naw, fuck wit' her," replied Reesie. "You know that shit wasn't cool at all, dawg. You shoulda kept it real."

"Yeah, big bro," stated Mya.

"Talk to her fo' me, Baby girl," Keke said with a confounded look on his face.

"I ain't got nothin' to do wit' that, Keke. Sorry! But I still love ya."

"Whateva', Baby girl," Keke said, walking away and waving his hand.

Nutcase was waiting on Libra when she returned. "Beautiful, what took you so long? Is everything okay?" Nutcase asked, showing serious concern.

"Yeah, I was talkin' to someone I know. Sorry to have kept you waitin'," Libra said, rubbing his back and giving him a small peck on the cheek. Libra knew Keke was looking. They enjoyed the rest of the show and then it was party time.

The DJ was hot tonight. The comedians were having a good time. Libra enjoyed Nutcase's company and all the affection he showed her. Mya and Gemini danced to every song. Even Reesie and Lorenzo danced a few times. Ton-Loc and Tiffany left after the show. Keke watched Libra the whole time, sipping his grey goose and cranberry juice.

The DJ slowed the music down. He played *Good Girls* by Joe. To everyone's surprise, Keke walked over to where Nutcase and Libra were and said, "I don't mean to be rude or show disrespect, but can I have this dance?" Libra looked at Nutcase, then back at Keke, and said nothing.

Nutcase said to Keke, "It's up to the lady."

"You don't mind?"

"No. I don't mind. You know where to find me," he said, looking at Libra and letting her know he was confident about himself. He then walked away. Libra wondered how a human being could be so caring and yet kill his own children, let alone the mother of his children. She needed a reality check.

"Keke, how the fuck you gon' intrude on me and my date? Did I intervene on you and yo' woman? No!" Before he answered, Libra said, "Once she made it clear who she was, I left it at that. So don't play me like that," Libra bitched, mad as a muthafucka'.

"Ladybug, you not me! And you had the same option to respond anyway ya wanted to. She's not my woman. She used to be," stated Keke angrily.

"Silly rabbit, tricks is for kids. So go find a girl, because I'm a woman, and as I stated before, you don't know what to do wit' me. I have a date and I don't wanna keep him waitin'."

With that said Libra left Keke on the dance floor and kept it movin' once again.

The DJ continued to slow it down. Lorenzo held Reesie's body real close to his. Both of them enjoyed the way each other body felt against one another. Just then, Caelin walked in the club with his boys, Don and Money.

The club was at its capacity. When they made their way through the crowd, they went straight to the bar. They all ordered Hulks, Hennessey and Hypnotic mixed together.

Caelin and his friends were big time hustlers and well known in the Lou. The crew reserved VIP, also. Walking to the table, Don spotted who he thought was Reesie, but he was not sure.

Don asked Caelin, "Fam, ain't that wifey on the dance flo'?" Don pointed in Reesie's direction. When Money saw Don pointing he knew immediately that it was

Reesie. Caelin made his way to the dance floor. Lorenzo saw him coming.

"Hey Reesie, here comes yo' man."

"Where?" Reesie asked, trying to remain cool. Before she could turn around, Caelin pulled her by the arm.

"Damn, Lay Lay! Hold up, baby," Reesie said as she stumbled through the crowd. Not wanting to make a scene, Reesie walked to the parking lot with him.

"Boo, what's up wit' that?" Caelin slapped Reesie in the face. "Ya kickin' wit' niggas! Ya know I don't get down wit' how that looks—my bitch chillin' wit' these ol' hater ass niggas. Ya know they want what I got, including you."

"Caelin, relax! Ain't nobody trippin' off you like that! Everybody knows I'm yo' woman. We were just having a good time, that's all. And by the way, since I'm yo' bitch, why did you have another bitch in our crib?" Reesie said to Caelin with her hands on her hips and her head tilted to the side, looking Caelin in his eyes.

"Huh?"

"Muthafucka', if you can huh, you can hear."

"Res I don't know what ya talkin' 'bout, man. You try'na change the subject, when it's really 'bout you, not me."

"Look, Caelin, we can talk about this later. The only thing I wanna do now is enjoy the rest of the night," Reesie said as she grabbed Caelin's hand to walk back inside.

He pulled away and said, "Res sit at my table baby."

Just so Caelin wouldn't make a scene, Reesie obliged his request. As they entered the club, Libra and Mya were on their way out.

"Where ya'll goin'?" asked Reesie.

"To check on you," replied Mya.

"You good?" asked Libra.

39

"I'm gutter," stated Reesie. "I'm gonna sit wit' my man, okay?"

"Okay," Libra said, walking back in the club with Mya behind her.

Libra and Mya could not stand the ground Caelin walked on. The only reason he was still breathing was because they knew Reesie loved the ground he walked on. If she ever wore a black eye again, Libra and Mya would have him disappear.

There was something about Caelin that troubled Mya. They sat at three different tables. Everything was going fine except for Caelin mean-mugging Lorenzo. Keke finally joined his boys.

"Damn, Lo, nigga's lookin' at you like he wanna talk to you 'bout sumthin'," Keke said, damn near drunk.

"Derrty, I ain't sweatin' these busters. They don't want no drama," Lorenzo stated while sipping his drink. "I got that heat like a hot summer day in the Lou. They don't want that." If you lived in St. Louis, you knew exactly what he was talking about.

The DJ played his last slow song for the night, *It Don't Hurt Now* by Teddy Pendergrass. Reesie and Caelin, Libra and Nutcase and Mya and Gemini danced to the song. "Ma, you goin' wit' me after we leave here?"

"Yeah, I can when I drop my girls off," Mya said, laying her head on his chest as they slow danced. Nutcase wanted to be with Libra, but he did not want to rush things. He thought he'd ask anyway.

"What you doing when you leave here?" Nutcase whispered to Libra.

"Nothin'. I'm goin' home," Libra said, swaying from side to side with her arms around Nutcase's neck.

"I would like for you to spend the night with me, if you don't mind," Nutcase stated in a deep tone that turned Libra on.

"I don't mind at all, Tyron," Libra mustered in a sexy tone of voice.

The night came to an end, and the club was about to close.

Caelin told Reesie, "Gon' on home and I'll meet you there. I have to drop off Money and Don, okay Boo?"

"Yeah, Lay." She had no intentions on going home tonight or any other night. She was leaving Caelin for good and the slap confirmed that decision.

Mya was kicking it with Gemini once she dropped Libra and Reesie off at home. She wanted things to remain on the down low with her and Gemini. They did not want to reveal their involvement at this time. They always hung out together, so it was no big deal seeing them together as much.

Keke wanted to approach Libra, but he knew she had no words for him. He did not leave alone. He left with some big booty chick from the Peabody Projects.

Libra thought to herself, a*s fine as he is, he love them ghetto ass bitches, but to each its own* and quickly discarded the thought of Keke from her mind.

Mya, Libra and Reesie were exiting the parking lot when they heard six loud gunshots. "Fuck! I hope that's not Caelin drunk ass," stated Reesie.

At that very moment, she turned around in the back seat of the car and looked out the window and saw Don fall flat on his face.

"Stop the car, Mya! Don just hit the ground!" Reesie yelled from the top of her voice. Mya pulled the car to the side of the parking lot. Reesie jumped out the car and ran to Caelin who was running to Don.

"Res go home now! Get the fuck away from here! I'll call ya."

Caelin turned Don over and saw the blood dripping down his face. He had a bullet hole in the center of his head.

"C'mon baby, hold on, ya strong nigga! We're five minutes away from DePaul Hospital. Don't let me down." Caelin had tears falling down his dark face as he spoke.

Money pulled the truck around and Caelin put Don's limp body in. Money sped down St. Charles Rock Road to the hospital. When they reached the hospital Don was pronounced dead. Caelin and Money couldn't bear the news. They only had revenge on their minds.

"Money, it's like that fo' them niggas," Caelin said, outraged.

"Yeah, all those niggas must die, starting wit' that bitch ass nigga, Lorenzo."

"Just let me at that ho ass bitch Lo. I got two bones to pick wit' him, one fo' my bitch and one fo' my man. Killin' two birds wit' one stone! Yeah, that's what's up."

His cell phone vibrated and interrupted his conversation.

"What's up, Boo?"

"How's Don?" Reesie asked, concerned.

"He didn't make it, Res," Caelin said very sadly.

"Baby, I'm sorry to hear that. Where you at? I need to be wit' you."

Reesie knew Caelin had murder on his mind. She could hear it in his voice, and she did not want to be around him while he was in that state.

"Nah, Res. I'm gutter. I'ma have Money drop me off in a minute. We have to take care of some biz'ness right now. I'll see ya in a bit, okay?"

"Yes, baby. I love you," Reesie said, feeling her man's pain.

"I love you too, Res," Caelin said as he disconnected the call.

Chapter 6

Caelin (Lay Lay) Ross

Caelin "Lay Lay" Ross was a very angry creature, and all so heartless. He was an only child. He'd grown up alone, feeling like it was him against the world, like Tupac. At the tender age of five, he'd seen an old friend of the family kill and shoot his mom in cold blood. His daddy was addicted to heroin and owed the dope man. He owed him a nice piece of change.

Bones is what they called his father. Caelin loved his father despite everything he'd done. He could not take the place of Patrice Ross. From the short time she had been in his life, he could remember all the wonderful things about her. She had long, wavy black hair. She had very pretty eyes and a nice figure. When Caelin lost his mother, life became overwhelming.

Responsibility was a must in the Ross household. Caelin was taught it at an early age. Bones provided everything he needed. He also showed him how to grind. All through Caelin's teenage years, he stayed into trouble. After a while Bones was fed up with his shit.

Caelin did a lot of things with Bones. They sold dope together, fucked the same women together. They even got high together. Bones had a girlfriend name Neshia. Neshia was a part of Caelin's life since his mom's death. She was the only other woman he trusted since Patrice. As Caelin got older, Neshia did things step moms didn't do. She was his first bit, his first piece of pussy.

Neshia, Bones and Caelin were smoking a premo and drinking Yak straight. Bones called it a night and went to bed. Neshia followed Bones to the bedroom and sucked his dick. Bones never wanted to fuck her, because she had some fire jawbone. That's what he fell in love with.

After Bones threw up in Neshia's mouth, he went to sleep. Neshia went back into the living room were Caelin remained. She walked over to him, bent down and unbuckled his pants. Caelin tried to stop her, but she was too aggressive. He didn't want his daddy to know what was about to go down and whom it was going down with.

"Caelin, relax. You know you want yo' dick to throw up," Neshia said seductively.

"Yeah, I do, but ya the wrong person to do that. My dad won't allow this, if he knew."

"How you know? Maybe he set this up."

"Yeah the fuck right!" Caelin bitched looking Neshia up and down.

Neshia continued to be presumptuous, and before long she had Caelin's dick down her throat. Caelin fucked Neshia mouth like he was fucking her pussy. She had a lot of dick in her mouth. She handled it like a pro.

"Oooh, damn girl, suck this dick." Caelin pumped harder holding her head. "Shiit!" Caelin said about to explode. "Swallow my baby, ya nasty bitch." Caelin wasn't finished with her. "Turn around!" He said to her as she wiped her mouth. Caelin thought Neshia had the best pussy in the world. Of course he would. It was the first piece of pussy he'd ever had.

When Caelin finished laying the pipe down, Bones walked in the living room and said, "Son, did you enjoy that? Nes got a mouth on her, don't she?" Caelin looked shocked as hell. He didn't know how to respond.

"Look old man. I didn't mean any disrespect." Caelin stated to his dad.

"Son it's okay, you can fuck her anytime you wanna, can't he, Nes?"

"You didn't know. Anyway he wants to," Neshia said as she walked to the bathroom.

From then on he fucked her whenever he wanted to and any other woman of his dad's. Caelin fell in love with Neshia. When she didn't oblige his requests, he beat the shit out of her. Neshia wore black eyes like she wore her panties and bras.

Caelin and Bones went to re-up. Their usual connections went bad, so they hooked them up with their peeps. Caelin was taught at an early age not to trust anyone, and he didn't. If things didn't go as planned he didn't mind killing even his own father. They always took Neshia along to test the product. Everything went fine on that trip.

Bones and Neshia were setting up shop one day when they were robbed. Bones was too stoned to protect their fortune. Caelin was out taking care of business on the other side of town, the dirty south. This stash house was the moneymaker, and they took everything. Caelin got a call from Neshia informing him that Bones had been shot and was in the hospital. Neshia had black eyes and busted lips, which was nothing unusual for her.

Caelin was determined to fine out who robbed him of his riches. He swore to God he would put them to sleep. He put that on Patrice and he never burned her grave unless it was going down and please trust, and believe it was.

Once he reached the hospital, he questioned his dad over and over again. Bones's response was the same, but something just didn't sit well with Caelin. He knew just the person to ask if he wanted to know anything.

Caelin saw Jokah sitting on his porch. "Hey Jokah, what's good?" The two men gave each other dap. "I need sum' info. I know ya know who robbed me for my riches. I got a grand fo' ya. Jokah, I know ya know. I really expect fo' ya to help me on this one. Ya got two days to decide. Here's five hundred now, and you'll get the other five when ya come clean. Cool!" Caelin said giving Jokah the money.

"Cool "Jokah replied.

Jokah found Caelin and Don smoking a blunt on his porch a few days later. "Lay Lay, let me holla at ya, young blood."

"Dawg, whateva' ya gotta say ya can say in front of my man, Don," Caelin said, passing Jokah the blunt.

"Look here, young blood. Dem cats from the north side's the ones got ya. All dem lil cats was at The Harlem Tap Room on Dr. Martin Luther King Drive last night talkin' 'bout this lick they came across wit' the help of two dope fiends."

Caelin and Don looked at Jokah intensively while he continued to tell them the story.

"Jokah, who are the dope fiends?"

"Young blood, ya know it was that ol' scandalous bitch of yo' dad's, and he had a hand in it, too. Now young blood, when ya go haul ass come correct, 'cuz dem cats roll deep. Ya understand'? Here's the address to the man in charge, but first deal wit' that bitch."

Caelin didn't like Jokah talking about Neshia that way, but he knew he had to deal with the situation.

"Good lookin' out Jokah, 'preciate ya. Here's seven hundred dollars. Go do sumthin' wit' yo'self."

"Anytime, young blood. Keep yo' head up. Ya too, Don. Now go handle yo' biz'ness. Start at home first, if ya know what I mean," Jokah said walking away.

The information Jokah dispensed fucked Don up but not Caelin. Bones had always told him to trust no one. Caelin was more disappointed that Neshia and Bones would do this to him. When all was said and done, they would pay. Don and Caelin sat on the porch a few more hours and put their plan in effect.

Caelin went home and found Neshia there. He acted as if everything was okay, and she did, too. Caelin and Don went into the kitchen to fix them something to eat. Neshia walked in the kitchen and saw them eating, but it wasn't what she'd cooked.

"Baby, I cooked. You want me to fix ya'll a plate?"

"Nah, we good. We need sumthin' light on our stomach for what's 'bout to go down."

Neshia looked at Caelin strange but disregarded the statement.

Neshia was in the bedroom, lying across the bed. Caelin walked in and lay across the bed and she put his nine on the nightstand. Don remained in the kitchen. Caelin moved closer to Neshia. "Nes, you okay? Look like yo' eyes goin' down. Tell me how those cats got in here."

"Lay, baby, when I went to the door, they pushed it open and hit me wit' the butt of the pistol."

"Do ya know them niggas?" Caelin said, as he looked Neshia in her eyes.

Neshia knew Caelin could be very treacherous, and she also feared for her life.

"Neshia answer the question. I'm not gon' ask yo' ass no mo'." Caelin's voice was very stern, and he had murder on his mind.

"Yeah, Lay Lay, it was those niggas from the north side," Neshia said with her head down.

Caelin had all the info he needed on the cats that'd robbed him. He was testing Neshia. "I tried to get to my strap, but one of the dudes knocked me unconscious."

"Neshia, ya know not to go to the muthafuckin' do' wit' out yo' strap. That's rule number one. Ya know the game. Don't fuckin' play wit' me. Don't play pussy and get fucked." Caelin became very angry as he talked to Neshia.

"I know but I was already over there by the door when I heard the knock."

"So what! I give no fuck about incompetence. That have cost me a lot, and someone must pay."

Neshia knew Caelin was serious. He no longer talked about the situation; all he knew is somebody took his riches and everybody involved will pay, starting with Neshia.

Caelin made Neshia think he forgave her and made love to her. It was something about the way he fucked her this day. He was more passionate then ever before. He caressed her a little more today than before. The lovemaking was exotic. Neshia performed every position she could think of to satisfy this man; not knowing this would be the last time she would ever do this.

When Neshia sucked on Caelin's manhood, he didn't release in her mouth like he usually did. He removed her head and asked her, "Nes turn around." She did as she was told. "I want some of this ass hole."

"Don't you need some lubrication?" Neshia asked as she turned around.

"Naw," Caelin said positioning Neshia body.

"Baby, yes you do," Neshia said almost at a whisper.

"Bitch, no I don't! Take this dick. Ya took my loot."

Caelin talked to Neshia through closed teeth. He became more forceful with her, pushing her head into the pillow. He forced himself into her asshole. The pain was excruciating and unbearable. Caelin continued to force himself inside of Neshia's ass. She screamed and cried for dear life, but that didn't stop him. Every time she screamed he punched her in the back of the head and pushed her face into the pillow harder.

"Don, come in here and let this bitch suck yo' dick. Do ya wanna fuck her derrty? Have it yo' way. This nasty bitch took my riches away."

"The hoe bitch can suck my dick. You keep yo' dick in her ass. Make this bitch pay for everythin' she did and was about to do."

"Bitch ya heard what he said. Lift yo' head and get down like ya live."

Neshia obliged their request despite all the pain that was inflicted on her. Both guys got their nut off and had more for her. Caelin got an orange extension card and beat her all over her body. When Caelin got tired, he and Don tied Neshia's bloody body up, not knowing if she was dead or alive. They put her in the trunk of the Taurus. He didn't care if she was dead or alive.

Caelin and Don parked the car in the garage at Don's house and stayed at the hotel for the night. Caelin was ready to deal with Bones. Bones was released from the hospital the next day. The duo picked Bones up. He was happy to see Caelin. As they rode, Bones noticed they were taken a different route.

"Son where we goin'?" Bones asked with a perplexed look on his face.

"To hell if we don't pray," Caelin stated sarcastically.

"That is so very true, but where are we goin' now?"

"Ya goin' to yo' grave ol' dope fiend ass, wanna be father. Ya told me trust no one. Ya forgot to tell me not to trust yo' no good fo' nothin' ass. That bitch Neshia will join ya. Say good night and I hope ya can swim."

Caelin shot Bones three times in the head. Don shot Neshia three times in the head but she was already dead from the abuse she received the night before. They threw the bodies in the river and continued their murder mission.

They knew their victims' hang out was O'Fallon Park on West Florissant St. When they arrived, they spotted them immediately. Don parked the car across the street from the park. Caelin and Don recognized their victims.

Caelin carried a nine-millimeter and a four five. Don carried a .357 and glock. Caelin and Don approached both guys sitting on the bench.

When they got closer, Caelin said to them, "Say good night muthafucka'," and blew their brains out. The guys were unprepared for their deaths. When they fell to the ground, Caelin and Don took everything they had in their pockets and walked away as if nothing had happened. They collected six thousand dollars and some jewelry. It wasn't close to the amount of money that was taken, but Caelin got satisfaction from their deaths.

Caelin and Don went back to Caelin's house and set it on fire. Caelin figured since Patrice was gone, he didn't need the house anymore. The only other woman he loved had betrayed him. His own flesh and blood had deceived him. He didn't need any more bad memories, and that's what the house represented to him. He and Don wanted to relocate and that's what they did. They continued to make their money. Bones left a healthy insurance policy.

The last thing he felt he needed to do was get a tattoo that said: TRUST NO ONE. The only person he trusted was Don, and it had its limitations, but he knew Don had his back and was down for whatever.

Chapter 7

Luv at First Sight!

Reesie became exceedingly indecisive about leaving Caelin after the news about Don. She knew he would need her, but she couldn't take the mental or physical abuse anymore. His temper was like a firecracker. It exploded at any given time when lit, and anything could trigger that explosion. Reesie got mad love for Caelin and she new that a resolution was needed for this situation. Reesie loved Caelin with all the breath in her body, but leaving him would be the best thing for her to do. If Reesie stayed, she knew her life would end.

Reesie revealed the news about Don's death to Libra and Mya when they reached the house. Silence fell amongst the girls for a few seconds.

Libra broke the silence with a prayer. "Ya'll bow ya'll heads." Mya and Reesie did as Libra instructed.

Libra prayed, "Lord Father God. I come to you tonight asking you to look down on us and heal some hearts. My Father, a man has lost his life in this wicked world. Lord, I know you said don't question you and I will not. Just please, Lord, watch over the hearts that's hurting and mend them. Father God, please give Reesie the strength and courage and adversity to satisfy her needs in life. Show her how to love herself again. Lord, you said we had not because we ask not. Lord, I'm asking you in Jesus' name. Amen. Amen."

Libra finished the prayer and looked at Reesie. Reesie had tears rolling down her high-yellow, freckled face.

"Boo, don't cry. That man upstairs got yo' back. We touched and agreed and it shall be done," Libra said, wiping the tears off her friend-sister's face and giving her a hug.

Mya had excused herself to the bathroom after the prayer. When she re-entered the room, she immediately joined in on the group hug. The friendship between the ladies has developed since the third grade. They had been through some things with each other, good and bad, but not once had they turned their backs on one another. They were each other's support system. Respect was the key to their friendship, the way they cared and loved one another. They were always mistaken for sisters coming from the same womb. They were like TLC, and the only thing that could keep them apart was death. Yeah, they all lived their lives how they wanted to, but never did that stop the friendship and bond.

Everything else was insignificant to Reesie if it wasn't about the almighty dollar. That's not saying she didn't give a fuck about nothing or nobody, but if you are a nigga, you'd better come correct, and Caelin "Lay Lay" Ross was that nigga.

The first night that Caelin met Reesie, he gave her a thousand dollars. Reesie was leaving her night class at St. Louis University (SLU). She stopped at the St. Louis Bread Company on South Grand to get a turkey club sandwich. She requested everything on her sandwich. Caelin had ordered already. After the orders were received, Caelin held the door open for Reesie.

"Thank you," Reesie said, walking out the door without looking back.

"That's no problem, Boo," Caelin said, enjoying every curve on Reesie's body. "Hot Girl!" he called out.

"Who? Me?" Reesie said turning around pointing to herself.

"Yes, you. I need to know yo' name, so I can call ya tonight," Caelin said confidently, knowing Reesie would give him the number—or would she?

The smell of her Happy Heart perfume made his manhood rise. The shape of Reesie's ass was a wonderful sight to Caelin. Reesie continued to walk when Caelin caught up with her. They were face to face. Caelin admired Reesie's beauty. Reesie continued to walk; only this time Caelin followed her to Street Side Records, trying to retrieve her number. Street Side records was located two doors down from the St. Louis Bread Company and next door to a Kinko's. Reesie went straight to the R&B session, with Caelin standing next to her. He got her undivided attention. He knew his music. R. Kelly's *12 Play* was the first CD he picked up. Reesie was very impressed. That was one of the CDs she'd come to get. She took the CD out of Caelin's hand and walked down the aisle. Caelin continued to follow her.

Reesie's hands were full with music and DVDs. She started to drop things. Caelin retrieved a small basket.

"Thank you again, sir." This time she smiled when she spoke to him.

"You quite welcome. Now can I have yo' number please?"

"Do you have a cell phone?"

"Uh huh!" Caelin said as he reached in the back pocket of his Rocawear jeans. Reesie gave him the number and he pushed the talk button to make sure it was the correct number. When he heard her phone ringing, he hung up.

"Yo' name please?"

"Reesie. Reesie Wright."

"Ms. Wright, when can I call ya?"

"Wheneva' you feel you wanna call."

53

"Can I please inquire about yo' man?" Before Reesie could answer Caelin asked. "Where yo' man at, hot girl? And keep it real."

"He's probable wit' yo' woman," said Reesie playfully. "Naw I don't have a man."

"Good, 'cuz I don't have a woman. I would love for ya to be my lady," Caelin said as he licked his full lips.

"You know what? All this conversation we're having, and I don't know yo' name."

"My name is Caelin Ross. My friends call me Lay Lay, and since I was so rude, let me pay for yo' things."

"Caelin, I wasn't finished yet."

"Well, take yo' time."

Reesie thought to herself, *Nigga you ain't said nothin' but a word.*

Reesie got *Brown Sugar* sound track, *The Mama Gun* by Erykah Badu, *My Life, The 411, Mary* by Mary J. Blige, the *Love and Basketball sound track for Libra, Jill Scott* and *12 Play* by R. Kelly.

Caelin saw Reesie approaching the register and he made his way there to pay for her purchases. Her total came to $135.60.

"Would ya like anythin' else, Ms. Wright?"

"No, that would be all Mr. Ross. Thank you."

Caelin paid for his purchases and walked Reesie to her car.

"Reesie, I know we just met and all, but I will like for ya to have a drink wit' me."

"When?"

"Now!" Caelin said, very serious.

"Where?" asked Reesie.

"Welch's in Wellston. Have ya heard of it?"

"Yeah, that's in da hood for real," Reesie stated.

"Well?" Caelin question Reesie.

"Well, what?" Reesie said before she realized it was in a nasty manner.

"Will ya join me? Please! Don't make me beg," Caelin, pleaded putting his hands together like he was praying.

"Maybe I'll go if you beg. Nah, I'm just kiddin'," Reesie said, showing her perfect set of teeth. "I'll go for a little while, okay?"

"That's what's up, Hot Girl. Follow me, okay?" Caelin said, walking to his car.

"Let's roll then, Hot Boy," stated Reesie, not believing she'd accepted his offer.

And with that, Reesie got in her clean white 1986 Cutlass Supreme and put her R. Kelly CD in and said to herself, *This is what it is.*

Caelin jumped into his gold SS Monte Carlo and got on Interstate 40 going west. He exited on Skinker and proceeded to St. Louis Avenue with Reesie following right behind him. The place was packed. The entire hood was there. Reesie and Caelin walked in through the back door. They sat at the bar closest to the door. Reesie thought Caelin's conversation was delightful. Caelin showed Reesie a great time. She had been uptight because of her final exams. She worried for nothing. Reesie was smart as hell, knowledgeable about both books and the streets.

Reesie let herself go with Caelin. She always kept it real, never passive. It was something about Caelin that warmed her. It was too real to be true. Caelin escorted Reesie back to her seat after the last slow dance. He watched as Reesie's hips swayed from side to side. You can't do anything but notice her hips; they are the first thing you see when Reesie's coming. The men loved Reesie's large hips alone with her bulky ass.

Caelin's head bounced with Reesie's ass, and she knew he was watching. She made it very pleasant for him, and for others that watched, as well. Reesie noticed the nasty stares she'd receive from the females. That just made her soldier strut even more enticing. Again, she said to herself, *This is what it is.*

Reesie and Caelin were having an intellectual conversation when Caelin heard a familiar voice approaching him.

"Ol' yeah! Ol' yeah, Lay Lay!" Once the female reached the table, she looked at Reesie from head to toe.

Reesie gave her a look back as if to say, "Eat yo' heart out. This is what it is."

The female stood next to Caelin and asked him, "You out trickin' wit' yo' little breezy? You don't know what I needed." She pointed in Caelin's face.

"And I don't give a fuck," Caelin said, never removing his eyes from Reesie.

"Every time you get a new bitch or a new piece of pussy, it's always fuck Sugar. You shole right, Caelin!"

Caelin was not in the mood for Sugar's shit tonight. He wanted a perfect night with Reesie. He would fuck her up if needed, and she knew that.

"Don't come over here, … " Caelin said, but before he could finish his sentence, Reesie intervened.

"Look I don't appreciate you comin' over here, disrespectin' me, callin' me outta my name. You don't know me from a can of muthafucka' paint; so don't come at me sideways. If this yo' man, then this is yo' problem, not mines home girl. Check yo' man, silly rabbit. Tricks is fo' kids!" Reesie stared as she rolled her eyes at the female. "Caelin check yo' bitch," Reesie said with her hands in her Fendi bag gripping silver, her 22.

Caelin had a feeling that Reesie was not the bitch to fuck with. He thought he would let Sugar write a check her ass couldn't cash. She had the right idea, but the wrong bitch. Sugar kept running her mouth, and out of nowhere

Reesie smacked her in the mouth with silver, knocking her two front teeth out. Before Sugar regained her balance, two others girls came running to her rescue.

Reesie pointed silver at the girls and told them, "C'mon, make my day, would you please?"

The girls stopped in their tracks immediately. They picked Sugar up off the floor. Caelin looked at Reesie apologetically and impressed. Caelin was feeling Reesie. He didn't want anything to stop him from getting to know her better.

The girls and Sugar continued to talk shit as they escorted Sugar out of the lounge. Reesie flinched at one of the girls and she jumped.

Reesie told Caelin, "These hoes don't want none. I don't even have to call my sistahs. I got this on lock down."

"What makes ya think ya gotta call anybody? Ya in good hands. I got yo' back. I see you're a ride or die chick. I like that 'bout ya, Ma. I also see ya have a no tolerance attitude. Does that mean ya not fuckin' wit' me?" Caelin said, sounding impressed.

"You know what Lay Lay?" Reesie said in a playful matter. "It will take more than some scary ass hoes to run me away. I can handle that."

"I see now that I have a Bonnie to ride wit' this Clyde. But check thickie-thick girl, take this thousand dollars and go get yo' nails and hair done. Buy ya an outfit and shoes, and don't forget the purse. I'ma take ya to a concert at Fox Theater tomorrow night, if that's okay wit' ya."

"What concert?" Reesie asked, surprised.

"Mary J. Blige, Joe, Jagged Edge and Avante. Ya know, the Budweiser Super Fest," Caelin informed Reesie.

"Ol' yeah! That's right," Reesie said, snapping her fingers like she had forgotten.

"This will be my way of makin' this night up to ya, Ms. Wright. Ya down?"

"Do Seagram's make gin?"

"That's what they say."

"Then it's a date." Reesie looked at Caelin seductively. They ended their date and Reesie took the money and the next day pampered herself as he'd requested.

Chapter 8

The Funeral

The day of Don's funeral, the weather was gorgeous and the temperature outside was seventy-five degrees. People came from everywhere to pay their last respects: the naughty north, da dirty south, da wicked west and east boogie. Donald Ray Jones was well known around the Lou. He was a very handsome guy. He resembled R. Kelly a lot, (so you know he was fine). His voice could raise the dead. It was exquisite. He was an all around genuine guy.

Caelin put Don away very nicely. He had the most beautiful coffin. It was white trimmed in gold. He had on a white Sean John suit with a white hat to match. The brim of the hat was folded in the coffin. Caelin and Money's suits were identical to Don's, with the white alligator shell toe shoes. Reesie also sported a white Sean John dress and hat with the matching alligator stilettos. This funeral was a fashion show. Caelin accompanied Don's family, and Reesie and Money accompanied Caelin.

Libra and Mya came to support their friend-sister, and also, Libra had to sing. Nutcase and Slick paid their respects, as well. Don and Nutcase had lived next door to each other as kids. Don became the kid Nutcase never knew when he and Caelin became inseparable.

Everyone gave his or her condolences and expressions of love. When it came time for Caelin to deliver his poem, there wasn't a dry eye in the church. Throughout the poem, Caelin had tears streaming down his dark chocolate cheeks.

Da Don!
There are no words that can express the hurt and pain that has been inflicted on me as well as the family.
But memories are everlasting.
The good and bad times we shared only last for so long.
But memories are everlasting.
The pictures we took can easily be torn into a million pieces, or burned in seconds.
But the memories are everlasting.
You were not only my friend, but also that biological brother my mother never had.
When we met we were like day and night, but ole so much alike.
We even allotted the same dreams and goals, but somewhere along this wicked journey, they were crucified.
As we travel this highway called life, we learned what's wrong and what's right. And you not being here, who's going to steer me right when I want to go left.
When I'm feelin' down, who's going to lift me up?
Well, I say that to say this.
Memories are everlasting, and I have so many.
I ask God, is there a heaven for a gangster? 'Cause Lord, one's on the way.
And even though you're not here in body, but always in mind. I love and miss you, man. You will never be forgotten.
And memories are everlasting.

Caelin made his way back to his seat. Even though Reesie knew she was leaving Caelin, she did not want to leave him in this state of mind. She held her arms open to him as he made his way back to his seat beside her. She did not know what to say to him, but she let him know she was there for him at that moment.

After the poem, you heard a lot of amens from the funeral attendees. Caelin walked to his seat, opening his suit jacket, showing the white T-shirt with a photo of Don, Money and him chilling at the Corey Spinks fight at the Savvis Center. Don was throwing up the STL sign. Pastor Johnson stood at the pulpit and said a couple of words of encouragement to the family.

"People of God, I want to smell my flowers while I'm still alive. You know, church we need to let our loved ones know how much we love them while they can still hear it and tell us they love us in return."

There were amens throughout the church again.

"We are not promised tomorrow, so let's live and put God first in our lives. Without Him, nothing is possible. Thank you, Jesus. Hallelujah! Let's not put off what we can do today for tomorrow, people of God. I know you're sad, but dry your eyes, because Brother Donald is in a better place."

Pastor Johnson raised her hands to give praises to the Lord.

"We're going to keep the order of the service. We're going call Sister Libra to give us a selection: *God say it, I believe it, I'm going to take him at his word.*"

As Libra made her way to the microphone Pastor Johnson said, "C'mon let's give the Lord a hand praise church!"

Libra had the entire church standing to their feet when she sang that song. She looked beautiful in her white Prada bell-bottom suit, with the white Prada boots. Nutcase admired her beauty from afar. He realized he was in church and quickly discarded the nasty thoughts out of his mind. He had to regain his composure.

After Don was laid to rest, Libra and Mya took some food they'd cooked to his mother's house. Mrs. Jones was a very nice person and beautiful for being in her fifties. They cooked turkey and dressing, candy yams, greens, hot water corn bread and fried chicken. Mrs. Jones accepted the food and asked them to stay, but they declined.

Reesie decided that she would stay with Caelin. But he informed her that he would be leaving for the neighborhood lounge, Sadie's. He wanted to have him a drink. He told her she could leave with Libra and Mya. He didn't have to tell her twice.

Mya drove Reesie's truck to Libra's and her house. Reesie sat in the back seat very quietly.

"Mya, put *sumthin' in the air*," stated Libra.

"It's at home. I didn't wanna bring that stuff in the Lord's house, Scales!"

"Girl, my bad. You right."

Reesie broke her silence. "Ya'll, I'm leaving Caelin. I'm tired of this grimy ass dude."

"You know you are more than welcome to stay wit' us. It's enough room," Libra said, turning her body to face Reesie in the back seat of her truck, looking very concerned.

"Libra!" Reesie called out to her frowning.

"What?" Libra said looking at her, puzzled.

"Girl, you know good n' well I can't stay at ya'll house. That's the first damn place he'll come looking."

"We don't have to open the door for that unhinged muthafucka'. Fuck him! He bleeds just like we do. What makes him think he's the only one that packs a piece?" Mya said, as she looked at Reesie though the rearview mirror.

"True, that." Reesie said looking back at Mya though the rearview mirror.

"Look! This ain't the time fo' that. Res, whateva' you wanna do, we got yo' back. Mya talk all that shit, but let a muthafucka' hurt you. She'll be the first bitch there," Libra said looking at both her friends-sisters.

"And you know this, man! You're my sistah girl." Mya glanced back at Reesie with a compassionate look on her face. "We all we got, derrty."

Entering the house, Libra picked up the remote control to the stereo and found Ghetto Boys title, *All I have in this world.* Mya was singing the song coming from the restroom, the first place she went after entering the house. Reesie went to the guest bedroom, which was really hers. The trio changed their clothes to something sporty, because they knew they were going in da hood and wanted to be comfortable. They always knew to dress for the occasion. That meant jeans and tennis shoes and sweats. The wicked west was no joke.

Libra drove her 300 to the lounge. Upon reaching the lounge, they saw all kinds of cars: Benz, Lexus, Hummer H2 and Old Schools. There were all kinds of makes and models of car parked outside. The ladies sat at Caelin's tables. Caelin had the Moet on chill. Reesie made sure she showed Caelin love before anyone else. She didn't want this human time bomb to explode. It could happen at any given time. Reesie hung with her girls most of the night. Caelin was drinking heavy and shooting pool. "Swappin' spit, talkin' bullshit," Caelin said to one of the fellows that was shooting pool with him.

"This me right here, blue ball in the side pocket, bet two bones."

"Do what ya do, derrty." The guy took the shot and made it. "That was luck, man."

"Call it what you wanna. That's two bones I didn't have," the guy said excitedly.

Reesie, Libra and Mya enjoyed each other's company, talking about people. The night was going well. Reesie wanted this day to be over so she could go on with her life without Caelin. She knew it was easier said than done. The DJ played the Martin Luther King slide, and the ladies went to the dance floor. Mya could do every electric slide invented. She guided Libra and Reesie through the dance.

Keke, Gemini and Lorenzo walked into the lounge. Reesie noticed them at the bar. Reesie got Mya and Libra's attention and they exited the dance floor. "This is just what the fuck I need. I knew this was too good to be true."

"Res you can't worry yo'self about Caelin and his actions. We can't stop them from comin' in a public place. Shit, Keke is the last person I wanna see, but I can't stop him from comin' in here."

"Yeah, I know Scales, but I don't want any drama and confusion."

"Ya'll wanna leave? We can go home and chill," Mya said as she looked at Gemini talking to her friends.

"Yeah, that's cool. Let me go talk to Caelin. Give me a sec."

Reesie excused herself from her friends and spoke with Caelin.

"Lay Lay, you 'bout ready to leave?"

"Naw, I'm good Boo. Ya can meet me at home later. I'm straight."

"I hope you're not drivin'. You are in no condition to be behind the wheel." Caelin still hadn't noticed Keke and his crew. Finally he turned around and saw them.

"That's why you're ready to leave. Ya think I'm fin'ta get on dem nigga's head," Caelin said to Reesie. At this point, his words were slurred.

"Naw Boo, I'm just tired. Baby, let that shit rest. This is Don's day. Let him have peace today. Caelin, I'm not sayin' don't handle yo' buz'ness, but not today, baby." While Reesie spoke to Caelin, she rubbed his arm and back, trying to relax him.

"Ya right, baby, I'm about to blow this joint when I finish this game of pool."

"We're about to leave too, okay Lay?" Reesie said to Caelin giving him a real passionate kiss.

"See ya later, and I love ya, Ms. Wright."

"I love you too, Mr. Ross," Reesie said to Caelin, exiting the spot, winking her eye at Lo. Mya and Libra spoke to the guys and the trio kept it movin'.

Chapter 9

Tha Trip

Libra and Nutcase were spending a lot of time together. Libra's birthday was in a couple of weeks. She and her sisters were going to Chicago and New York on a shopping spree, however Keke got knowledge of this trip. The day they were leaving, a guy from Nettie's Florist knocked on her door. This was the last thing Libra expected. She retrieved her Old Navy purse from the couch and tipped the guy very generously.

"You have a good day, Libra," said the deliveryman pleasantly.

"You have a better one," Libra replied, closing the door behind the guy.

Libra wondered how the delivery guy knew if she was Libra or not, and then realized she'd signed her name. She'd received a huge card with a smaller envelope attached. Libra read the card and was drawing to the end of it when it said: FRIENDS FO'EVER.

She read the other card and wanted to call Keke and thank him for the gift, but deep down inside, she wanted to see Keke as well. Libra contemplated about rather or not she should call Keke. Her consciousness ate away at her, and she gave in. She finally picked up the phone and dialed his cell number.

She talked to herself out loud as the phone rang. "Why does this man have me so nervous?"

As she put the phone to her ear she heard Keke greet her. "Hey Ladybug!"

"Hey yo'self," Libra said with a smile.

"What's good, Mommy?"

"Nothin'. Slow motion, big daddy," Libra said, sexier than imagined.

"Damn, Ma! Why you say it like that?" Keke asked excitedly.

"Like what?"

"Like that, baby," Keke said, much calmer than before. "What's good wit'cha, sweetheart?"

"I'm blessed. What about you?"

"Thinkin' 'bout you." Keke's voice made Libra melt the way cotton candy melted in her mouth.

"I'm glad to hear that, Keke."

"Fo' sho'. Look baby, I was thinkin'. I really wanna see you, Ladybug. I miss you. The last time we were together and had our intimate moment, I've been prayin' fo' the day ever since. I'm only human, and we all make mistakes. You supposed to learn from them. Libra, I've learned my lesson. Experience is the best teacher."

If only Libra could see Keke's face at that moment! She would have known how truthful he was.

"I'm on my way to Chicago."

"You're not gon' yet?" Keke said to Libra very aggressively.

"I know, but the girls are on their way to pick me up to hit the highway."

"Ladybug, tell Baby girl to stop in da hood befo' ya'll hit the highway. You know what, Ladybug? Don't worry 'bout it. I'll call Baby girl myself. You just be ready when she comes to get you."

Keke had every intention of finding out what hotel the ladies were residing at.

"A'ight, you win. I'll be ready, but I can only stay a few minutes."

"That's cool, Ma."

And with that said, they disconnected the call. Mya and Reesie walked through the door five minutes later. Mya

was on her cell phone, running to the bathroom sayin',
"Um huh. Okay. Got it. No problem."

"I hope yo' slow ass ready, Scales," Reesie said
walking to the kitchen getting her something to snack on.

"Bitch, I'm ready. You don't know nothin' 'bout
me. I've been ready like yesterday," Libra said, sticking her
tongue out at Reesie. They both laugh.

"Scales, you're in a good ass mood. Who you let
rock yo' boat?" asked Reesie.

"The pissie bitch talked to Keke, and he wants her
to stop in da hood befo' we leave. He also sent her some
roses," Mya stated, coming from the bathroom, revealing
all of Libra's business.

"Damn, Madlock, get you some buz'ness and get
outta mines."

"Lemme read the card. Let's see how romantic he
is. I hope he has more than good looks," Reesie stated
nastily.

"Let's get these bags in the truck so we can hit the
road. You's a nosy heifer," Mya said to Reesie.

"You know you wanna read it too, tramp."

They all broke into a hysterical laugh.

The ladies packed their bags in Mya's baby blue
Trail Blazer truck and headed for the wicked west side.
When they arrived, Keke, Gemini, Ton- Loc and Lorenzo
was playing basketball in the driveway of Gemini's house.
Keke was looking scrumptious to Libra. She could have
stop breathing when she saw him. Keke walked over to
Libra and gave her the most intimate hug ever. She admired
his baby blue Ecko sweat suit with the baby blue Timbs.
His face was well groomed and his haircut was fresh as
ever alone with a trimmed goatee.

"Damn, Ladybug! You wearing the hell outta' those
Seven jeans. Girl, you look good as fuck. You sexy as hell
to me. You can make a blind man see."

Libra's hair was styled in a feather bob hairdo. She did look good in her Seven outfit with her fresh pair of Airmax tennis shoes. Keke grabbed the back of her neck and they had a tongue war.

Mya and Gemini held each other rather close, also. Mya rocked her Polo sweat suit and a pair of Polo tennis shoes with a flipped ponytail.

"Baby girl, I miss you already. How long you gon' be gone?" Gemini asked in his deep baritone voice.

"We'll be back in a week. We're stayin' at the Embassy Suit Hotel on Lake Shore Avenue. I want you to come wit' me," Mya told Gemini, rubbing her hands through his locks.

"Ma, this about yo' girls b-day, right?" replied Gemini.

"Naw, this is about us, Poppy." Mya looked at Gemini seductively.

"Keke wanted to come along, so he had Rhonda to reserve our rooms. Mya, I'm feelin' the shit out of you in more ways than one. We both are grown, why do we have to hide? I don't think we should have to hide our relationship. I love everythin' about you. Baby girl, I'ma man and I take care of mines, so roll or get rolled over."

Gemini looked Mya in the eyes without blinking, letting her know he was serious. He pulled Mya as close as possible to him, until her nipples poked him in his chest. He affectionately kissed her and she returned the kiss, wrapping her arms around his neck, not giving a damn who saw them. His kisses had her in ecstasy. They broke their embrace when they heard the others clearing their throats.

Reesie was hesitating about Lorenzo. All she knew was that she was attracted to him in the worst way. She couldn't shake this feeling she had. The feeling was established the night Don was killed, and even though she'd made up her mind to leave Caelin; she wanted to go about the situation cordially.

"Reesie, how you doin'?" Lorenzo asked.

"I'm a'ight, Lo. What about yo'self?"

"I'm good."

"That's good to hear," Reesie stated in a playful matter.

"You're a hot commodity in those Fetish jeans, and they look hot on you, Lil Mama."

"You think?"

"On the real, Reesie," confirmed Lorenzo.

"No, on the fake," commented Reesie. "I'm just playin, but naw. Thanks, sweetie." Reesie had a real sense of humor at times.

"So ya'll goin' to the Windy City and the city that never sleeps, huh?"

"Yeah, Scales wanna go shopping for her birthday."

"Do you mind if an admirer comes along?" Lorenzo asked with hesitation.

"This is a free country. You can do as you please," Reesie explained to Lorenzo.

"Say no more, it's a done detta."

Keke wanted his car washed before he hit the highway. He told the ladies to follow him to B&B car wash in Wellston. The fellows jumped in the Old School with the ladies right behind them riding up Martin Luther King Drive to Keinlen Avenue. When they arrived, it was packed. Keke knew the owner, Shane, and he immediately started washing the truck and car.

"While they waited for the vehicles to be washed, Mya and Reesie went to the store down the street to get some zoo-zoos and wham-whams for the road. The fellows went to the rice house and ordered something to eat. Libra sat in the waiting area of the car wash, reading the Flipside Newspaper and saw Nutcase in the paper representing the youth basketball tournament. He was head coach for the basketball team and had coached for two years. The Young Futures were undefeated. It was an all-year-around league, and Nutcase took out time to give back to the community. Seeing Nutcase in the paper with the team made Libra feel a sense of guilt. Libra knew Nutcase cared a great deal for her, and she was going out of town with Keke, who had a woman already. This situation was not part of Libra's element at all.

She kept telling herself, "I'ma be good," but she knew in her heart that was a lie and the truth wasn't in her.

The ride to Chicago was an excursion. The trio blew their brains out, smoking the hydro Keke had given them. When they reached the hotel, everybody went to their rooms. Libra's room was extravagant. Rose pastels met her at the door and lead her to the master bedroom. She had a dozen of white and yellow roses on each nightstand, with a note attached.

> *Libra,*
> *These are just a few words to describe such*
> *a wonderful person:*
> > *Loving*
> > *Interest*
> > *Breeds*
> > *Rare*
> > *Attributes*
> *Love me, Keke*

Libra had a big kool-aid smile on her face. After a few seconds, she snapped back to reality. She was about to get in the shower when Keke knocked on the door. She opened the door for Keke, and before he could enter the suite, she started kissing him passionately.

"Would you like to join me in the shower, Mr. Larkins?" said Libra flirtatiously, guiding Keke to the bathroom.

"Yes I would, Ms. Love."

When they reached the bathroom, Libra undressed Keke. She was mesmerized by the thickness of his dick. The only thing she could think of was how it would feel inside of her. Keke broke her thoughts.

"Ladybug let's get in the shower befo' the water gets cold."

"We got all night, baby."

"Fo' sho'," replied Keke.

Keke entered the shower first, reaching for her hand. He made sure the temperature was okay, and it was just right. He pulled Libra close to him.

"Baby can I ask you sumthin'?"

"Ask me anythin' you wanna," Libra said, looking Keke in his chestnut eyes.

"Are you happy?" he asked, rubbing her arm.

"Where is all this comin' from? And what does this have to do wit' anythin'?" Libra said, agitated.

"Everythin' Libra," Keke shot back at her.

"You shouldn't worry about Tyron. I'm not askin' 'bout Pooh."

Keke could tell Libra was getting upset.

"Libra, don't come at me wit' no damn attitude. I asked you a question 'cuz I wanna fuckin' know. I'm fallin' in love wit' yo' stubborn ass."

Libra turned her back to Keke. He walked behind her in the shower and pulled her close to him by her waist. All she felt was his dick against the small of her back. He bent her over and inserted his index finger in her twinkie. When he removed it, he licked all her love cream from his finger.

"Baby I want to make love to you," Keke said in a very low tone.

"I want you to make love to me," Libra said, breathing hard.

Keke sat down in the tub with the shower running.

"Ladybug, come put that monkey in my face." Libra did as she was told. Libra dog walked his face and he loved every minute of it. As Keke sucked her pussy she talked nasty to him.

"Suck this pussy, boy! Oooh-oooh, shit! Damn, Keke." The feeling was so overwhelming; she wanted to make him feel the same way he made her feel.

"C'mere, daddy."

Libra got on her knees and sucked Keke's dick like he never had his dick sucked before. They left the bathroom and kissed their way into the bedroom.

"Lay down," Libra said as she pushed him down on the bed and climbed on top of him. She put his legs in the air like a bitch and rode him. Keke couldn't believe the way Libra took control, but he didn't have a problem with it. He let her have her way with him. They made love for the next hour. Keke was everything Libra had heard he was, and more. She could see herself sexing him every day.

"Mya and Reesie wanted to eat. They called Libra's room.

Ring, ring!

"Scales, what are you doin'? We're hungry."

"I am, too. Where we goin'? Are ya'll ready?" Libra said, extremely exhausted.

"I don't know. Maybe we can go to Robinson Barbecue, but would you please bring yo' ass?" Mya said as they disconnected the call.

Libra placed wet kisses on Keke's face to wake him up. They got a quickie off, jumped back in the shower and headed out the door. On their way down to meet the others, all Libra could think about was what had taken place in her room, and she couldn't wait until they got back and continued were they'd left off at. She was like a dope fiend. She needed her next fix.

The next day, the fellows took the ladies on a wonderful shopping spree. The ladies purchased Prada, Chanel, Dolce and Gabbana, Gucci and Louis Vutton and a few other designers. The six of them went to Club Urban and had a beautiful time. Keke knew the owner, and he showed them much love. He and Keke did business together. The DJ was off the chain. Mya kept Gemini on the dance floor. Libra and Keke took several photos, along with the others. Reesie and Lorenzo shared conversation most of the night. The club was getting ready to close, and Keke wanted to make love to Libra again. Mya and Gemini played strip poker and smoked blunts all night. Reesie and Lorenzo continued their conversation from earlier.

Keke decided that he and Libra would take a walk around Lake Michigan.

"Baby, you feel like taking a long walk?"

"Around the park after dark," Libra said to Keke, singing a Jill Scott song to him.

"Fo' sho', Ladybug. Fo' sho'."

Keke had already decided that he would make love to Libra on Lake Michigan. He didn't know if she was spontaneous, but he would soon find out.

Walking around the lake, Keke carried Libra on his back. He placed his hands under her ass, and got his feel on from time to time. Libra didn't stop him. She was delighted. Libra hugged Keke's neck and kissed him periodically.

"Keke tell me why you're allured to me?"

Libra caught Keke off guard with the question. They stopped walking and Libra got down from his back.

"Look at you, Ma. Who wouldn't be allured to you?"

Keke's eyes searched Libra's entire body for flaws, but he couldn't find any. Flawless! They stared into the sky. The night was perfect.

"Ladybug, what do I have to do to have you to myself?"

Libra brushed the question off. "Baby, the sky is beautiful. I just wanna enjoy this time wit' you."

Libra stood in front of Keke on her tiptoes to kiss him. He participated in the kiss. He tried to resist, but couldn't. He pushed her away, but coming closer, she kissed him again.

"Ladybug, will you answer my question?"

She kissed him again, and this time, he let himself go with her, because the chemistry between them was overpowering. He laid her down on the grass by the lake and raised her Chanel dress above her thighs and inserted his finger and worked it around, playing with her clit. Libra enjoyed every motion of his hand. She rotated her hips with his strokes. She released all over his fingers and he removed them and placed each one of them in his mouth, one by one, as if he was sucking on a sucker.

Libra liked the extracurricular activities she and Keke engaged in. Despite the ordeal at the Royal Palace with Pooh, at this point Libra gave no fuck. All she knew was she loved the way this man made her feel. He represented in the fashion of the truly gifted, and as he made love to her, he talked to her.

"Gimme' this pussy!" Keke said as he stroked.

"Here, get it! I'm givin' it all to you. Take it." She wanted him to feel all of her.

"Make me know this dick good to you," Keke said as he bit his bottom lip frowning.

"Can't you tell from the way I'm fucking you?"

Keke didn't like to use the word fuck, because he knew he would never fuck Libra. He would always make love to her when the time was right, and the time had come.

"Ladybug, look at me. Don't never ever forget this. We will never fuck. I will always make love to you. I wanna make sure you are satisfied in every way possible."

Their bodies exploded in ecstasy, and all they could do was hold each other. They knew it would end soon. Keke also knew Libra was a down ass bitch, and he like that in her.

The next morning, Keke made plane reservations for the six of them to fly to New York. The ladies were elated. As soon as the ladies touched down, they purchased Cartier watches for the fellows with their names engraved on them. Keke knew that he and the fellows had business to handle, so they wouldn't be able to spend as much time with the ladies as they would have liked to. He informed Libra of his plans. Here was another time he would see if she were his soldier.

"Ladybug, the fellas and I got mad bit'ness to handle. You know, I want nothin' more than to spend this time together, but I will make it up to you. Please believe me." Keke kissed Libra on the forehead.

"Keke, that's cool. Mya, Reesie and I can hang out. You know, do girl stuff. Like go shoppin'."

"Here, take this five grand and enjoy yo'self. I'll see you by dinnertime. Ladybug, I'm falling in love wit' you. As I stated once befo', when I love, I love hard."

"Well sweetheart, we gon' take this one day at a time. What's meant to be will be. That's what they told me. Now, go handle yo' buz'ness before I rape you."

Libra called her friends after Keke left. *Ring, ring!*
"Hello."
"What's up, Baby girl?"

"Nothin'! Wanna get my fuck on, but Gemini had to make a move," Mya said, disappointed.

"I'm sure you fucked enough in Chicago."

"Yeah, I did, and it was off the chain. That's why I wanted some mo'."

"Well, let's go kick it for my birthday," Libra said, very excited.

"Okay. I'll be in yo' room in two."

"I got to call Reesie. You think she let Lo knock dem boots?" Libra said to Mya, whispering.

"Shit, why don't you ask her?"

"Bitch, you know she's private!" Libra replied, yelling at Mya though the phone.

"I'll ask her, then. They were together this mornin' and sat together on the plane. Maybe she did release some stress and tension.

"That's good if she did. Get at me in a minute." And with that, they disconnected the call.

Ring, ring!

"Yeah!" Reesie answered the phone, out of breath.

"What are you doin'?"

"I just got outta the shower."

"We're about to get out like girls scouts. Get dress and let's roll."

"It's all good," Reesie confirmed, and they disconnected the call.

Libra drove the black Bonneville Keke reserved for them. The trio went into every store on the strip. They were in the Chanel store when an impressive guy approached them. He had been conscious of the trio since they walk through the door. His persona was delighting. He was also dressed conservative, like P. Diddy on the red carpet. The handsome species kept his eyes on Reesie. He proceeded to approach the ladies.

"Why this muthafucka' keep lookin' at us like we gon' steal sumthin'?" Reesie said to Mya, agitated.

"Excuse me, ladies. I detected that you are not from around here. You, my lady, have an air about you that accentuates your whole being. I can see you are very business-minded. I can make you an offer you can't refuse," the gentlemen said, extending his hand to Reesie.

"Pardon my bluntness and correct me if I'm wrong. And if I'm wrong, I give you my most and deepest apology. I think we can do wonderful business together. My name is Taijeon Hendrix."

Reesie shook the guy's hand but was very dubious about his approach.

"Reesie Wright. This here is Libra and Mya, my sistahs. What is it that I can help you wit' or try to assist you wit'?"

"Now, please tell us what you want?" Libra said looking at him perplexed.

"Like I said once before, I know you all are not from around here, and I like to do business with people from other states. It's money everywhere to be made, and maybe if you can obey the rules once I explain, you can determine if this is for you," Taijeon said to the ladies looking extremely serious.

"Go ahead and state your proposal, please," Reesie suggested.

"Ladies a tree fell on my house and knocked it completely down."

Taijeon had the girl flustered at this point.

"Okay, a tree fell on yo' house. What do that have to do wit' me? I mean us?"

"You really don't understand do you?" asked Taijeon.

"No, so will you please break it down for us."

"You see I just received two hundred pounds of that purple haze and I need to get rid of it ASAP. I was letting it walk for sixteen hundred a pound but at this point I'm willing to take on chance on the three of you."

"Hold the fuck up! Rewind. How you gon' come to us like that. You could be the muthafuckin' police for all we know. We don't move like that pat'na," Libra stated to Taijeon.

Libra knew this guy wasn't the police, but she had to make sure. She needed to know what he wanted. The man seemed very interested in what he was presenting, so she let him finish his proposition.

"I'm willing to let you leave here with six pounds. And of that six, you all can have … three for yourselves! Bring me back $2600 off each pound, a total of $7800 in all. You can do what you like with yours, and after you prove your loyalty, I will plug you in with my connects."

Taijeon knew he'd put a great offer on the table, and Reesie wouldn't refuse. He knew she was going to take it.

"Why did you pick me? Do you know my life style, or did I represent myself to you as a hustler?" Reesie spoke to the guy skeptically. "What if I don't bring yo' money back?"

"We will cross that bridge when we come to it, and this is why we call life a chance—because we take so many of them," Taijeon said to the ladies, showing his pearly whites.

"We will have to give this some thought. Can we call you when we come to a decision and give us a number you can be contacted at? We'll get at you before we depart. You know everythin' that's good to ya ain't good fo' ya, and everythin' that's good fo' ya ain't good to ya. You understand what I mean, Mr. Hendrix?" Mya looked for anything that implied that this man is not sincere.

"I understand exactly. You can never be too sure. People are sheisty and grimy these days. Here's my card. Give me a call. What day are you all leaving?"

"In a few days," Libra said to the man, looking at him suspiciously. "You will hear from us sometime tomorrow. Is that okay?"

"That's fine," stated Taijeon.

He wanted to ask the ladies where they were staying, but he'd sprung too much on them already. The way they were acting, he would not get any details about their living status in the big city.

They went back to the hotel room to discuss the pros and cons of this offer. Libra said to her friends, "Ya'll know that's a whole pound we got to ourselves. The Lou has a drought on the goods. We can move that in a week. What do you think, Res? He made the offer to you but you know we're in this together."

Libra, Mya and Reesie sat around and waved their options.

"Why not do this? Like he said, life is a chance and I don't wanna sit around here thinkin' or sayin' to myself should 'a, could' a, would' a. That pound we have for ourselves is gutter. So what's it gon' be?" Reesie commented to her friends.

"I'm in," said Libra.

"Me, too! Reesie make that call first thing tomorrow morning," Mya said with excitement

"No doubt," replied Reesie.

The ladies heard the fellows coming. Keke let himself into Libra's room. Gemini and Lorenzo went to their rooms.

"Oh, my bad, I didn't know you had company," Keke said as he walked in the room and kissed Libra on her shining lips.

"That's okay. They were about to leave," Libra said, looking at Mya and Reesie.

"What's up, big bro? We're goin' out tonight?"

"Fo' sho, Baby girl. We gon' kick it tonight, 'cuz this is our last night here. The bit'ness we gotta take care of became overwhelming, so that means pleasure on hold. We can do whateva' ya'll wanna do."

"Keke, we are not leaving until Friday," said Libra with an attitude.

"I'm sorry, Ladybug. I wasn't implying that ya'll have to leave. Ya'll still can leave Friday."

"That's what we gon' do," Libra said angrily while rolling her eyes.

"Ladies, go get dress!"

Keke disregarded Libra's last comment and how she said it. Reesie and Mya exited Libra's room, sensing she was upset about Keke's departure.

Now that Libra's room was clear, Keke would see why Libra was upset all of a sudden.

"Baby did I say anythin' to make you mad at me?" Keke looked at Libra, baffled.

"How you gon' burn out on me like that?"

Keke thought she was sexier when she was mad. "Babe I told you I had some bit'ness to handle," he said as he kissed her neck.

"Boy, stop! You ain't gettin' none of this fire."

Libra knew she was lying. She was sitting on the edge of the king size bed when Keke stood in front of her. He bent down and pushed her back on the bed. She didn't resist him. She enjoyed everything he did to her and was about to do. They made love before they went out. It was the best five minutes Libra had ever had.

"Keke, I hope there won't be any problems when we get back to St. Louis."

"Why should it be? I know you gotta man and I'ma respect that, Ladybug."

"Keke you have someone, also," Libra said, rolling her eyes and neck at Keke as she spoke.

"C'mon, let's get out of here and enjoy ourselves on our last night together for now."

Keke didn't want to get into that discussion with Libra at the time, because he really didn't know how he was going to handle the situation when he saw her with Nutcase. With that, they kept it movin'.

They went to a Jamaican Club. The atmosphere was hyped. The St. Louisian looked good to the New Yorkers. Mya got on the dance floor and did the chicken head and Neno Pop—the dances that had put St. Louis on the map. She was an excellent dancer, and the people knew where they were from because of the dances Mya did.

Reesie noticed Taijeon at the bar. They made direct eye contact. Reesie wondered if this man had been following her. If he thought about doing anything to her, he'd better think twice, because she had danger with her—a .38 snug nose, and she wasn't afraid to use it. She got Libra and Mya's attention. They followed her eyes, excused themselves and went to the restroom.

"Mr. Hendrix, are you followin' me?" Reesie asked him on her way to the restroom. Mya and Libra continued to the restroom. Mya couldn't hold it anymore.

"No, Ms. Wright. I own this joint. Did you see the name on the outside? Club Hendrix's?"

"Yes, I did." Reesie was upset with herself for not being more observant.

"Have you come to a decision yet?"

"My deadline is tomorrow, right?" Reesie asked him.

"Yes, it is."

"I will inform you about my decision tomorrow by noon. You have a nice day."

After the pleasantries, Reesie kept it movin' and said to herself, *This is what it is.*

The DJ played *Deep* by Black Street. Everyone slow danced and was having a good time. Then the DJ pumped *Best Friend* by Brandy. The trios made their way back to the dance floor. It was their theme song—*Friends Till Death Do Them Part.* Gemini noticed Taijeon and a person that looked identical to him. It was Sameon, his identical twin brother.

"What if you had a twin brother, Keke?" Gemini asked.

"Man, God knew what he was doin' when he created one of me. It would be hell to tell the captain," Keke replied to Gemini, and they laughed. Keke ordered his grey goose and cranberry juice and a Corona beer. He was feeling good.

"Lo, you hit that yet?"

"Fam, a man never kiss and tell," Lorenzo stated as he took a sip from his drink. He stared at Reesie as she conversed with Taijeon.

"That means 'Oh yeah!'" Keke shouted and gave Gemini dab.

Gemini and Lorenzo ordered themselves another Martell and Remy straight.

"Derrty, ya'll know the punk ass nigga Lay Lay think we knocked Don," Gemini confirmed. "We got to get at that clown real soon. He's one of those grimy niggas. You have to get him befo' he gets you. We gon' take care of him as soon as we touch down. Hold tight! That nigga is on the death wish list." He glanced towards the dance floor. "Here comes the ladies. Chill out."

"Reesie, do you know that guy over there by the bar?" Gemini inquired.

"I'm afraid not," Reesie stated, not wanting to look like she was lying.

"He must like what he see, 'cuz his twin is checkin' Libra out."

"What twin?" asked Libra.

"The guy by the bar. Look to yo' left."

Everybody followed Gemini's eyes. The girls were speechless. They really wanted to know what was going on with this guy. Reesie informed everybody that she was ready to leave. They finished their drinks and kept it movin'. As they exited the club, Taijeon winked his eye at the girls.

The next morning, the fellows left to go handle their business back in the Lou. Libra and Keke decided that they would keep in touch. Mya gave Gemini some fire neck before he departed. Reesie fucked the shit out of Lorenzo and shared things with him her two best friends-sisters didn't know, and would never know, because he would take what they shared to the grave with him. The fellows said their good byes and kept it movin'.

The ladies were dubious and suspicious about Taijeon's offer, but they knew it could be an accolade for them at the same time. Reesie thought she would contact Taijeon and confront him about his actions.

Ring, ring!

"May I speak with Taijeon please?"

This is Taijeon. How are you doing, St. Louis?" Taijeon asked in a pleasant voice.

"I'm blessed," Reesie responded. "Taijeon, why didn't you tell me you had a twin brother?"

"I didn't think it was important, you're doing business with me, not Sameon"

"That's his name, huh?" Reesie replied.

"Yup! That's his name."

"Taijeon, now that we have that out of the way, we're leavin' tomorrow and we've decided to take you up on yo' offer if it's still available. I also have a few questions about how will we get the product? I'm not takin' that shit back on the plane wit' us."

"Slow down, Tito. Damn! Sameon and I have a van with hidden compartments. We will drive to the Lou and make the drop personally. I heard the muthafuckin' police will lock you up and throw away the key. You can meet us at my safe house in U City, right off Olive Rd. Does that sound familiar to you?"

"Yeah, that's cool. I live in the Lou, so I know where just about everything's at," stated Reesie.

"You said I wouldn't have to deal with Sameon, but he's helping you deliver. You need to keep me informed on whom I dealin' wit' doin' this process, and I will do the same for you. Understan'?" Reesie informed Taijeon.

"You are right, St. Louis. As soon as ya'll touch down, call me at this number. I hope you can get back at me within three weeks, Ma," Taijeon said solemnly.

"Taijeon, when we meet again, I will have half of what I owe you. Thirty nine hundred, okay? I will have the other half in two weeks or before then. Everythins' kosher, now?" Reesie asked confidently.

"Everything good then, St. Louis. See you tomorrow."

They disconnected the call.

Reesie plugged Libra and Mya in on the conversation. They were pleased with the outcome. The trio decided to chill their last night in New York, but not Mya. She met this guy on the elevator and fucked him right there. She didn't care. She was from out of town, and he would never see her again—or would he? The next morning, the trio got in the Bonneville and headed to the airport. Keke had Mya's Trailblazer shipped home from Chicago.

Chapter 10

Da Big Birthday Bash

In the meantime, Nutcase was home planning the biggest birthday bash of the year. He had no problem with Libra taking a trip without him. That gave him time to wrap up last-minute details.

Mya and Reesie was a big part of planning the party also. Mya prepared the menu and Reesie did the decors. Nutcase spared no expense for those of them that were fortunate enough to receive an invitation. The party was by invitation only. Nutcase made damn sure of that. He hired the best security team money could buy. Libra had no idea this party was about to go down. The invitation read:

Hey it's a Libra thang. Come party with Libra a.k.a. Scales. Please respond by October 1, 2004. Also, indicate the number of guests that will accompany you and reply to the address above. Invitation must be shown upon arrival. Blessings.

The invitations were gorgeous. They were silver with pink writing and a picture of Libra's face surrounded by scales.

When Libra, Mya and Reesie touched down in the Lou at St. Louis Lambert Airport, Keke had Mya's truck waiting on them. Libra hadn't spoken to Keke since his departure from New York. She wanted it to remain that way, but Libra, being that one hundred percent real female that she is kept it real with herself. She knew she would have to have herself some Keke at all costs, whatever that may be.

"Scales, exactly what are we doin' for yo' birthday?" Reesie asked, entering on Interstate 70 eastbound.

"I don't know. Nutcase and I 'ma chill wit' ya'll and make this money out here," Libra said from the passenger seat, never removing her eyes from the photos of her and Keke.

"Res, when we gonna call ol' boy?"

"Mya, we need to get situated first. You know drop these bags at the crib," said Reesie.

"So you have decided to stay wit' us after all?"

"Nope! I'ma chill tonight. Then I'm at Mrs. Wright's crib. Caelin can't come there and clown. Mama will put that lead in that ass. She don't give a damn," Reesie said to her friends-sisters, laughing, and they knew it was true.

"That's cool then, Res," stated Mya.

The trio reached the house and made the call to Taijeon.

Ring, ring!

"What's up, New York?" Reesie stated in an upbeat manner.

"What's good?" Taijeon said in his New York accent.

"I called to find out where is the meeting spot."

"I see. You strictly business, St. Louis," Taijeon said, sounding impressed with Reesie's forwardness. "Meet me in University City in one hour on Olive and 82nd Street on the 7-11 parking lot."

"See you then," Reesie said, about to hang up.

"Reesie!" Taijeon said before she disconnected the call.

"Yes?" Reesie says calmly.

"Do you have what we talked about, inferring about the cake?"

"Taijeon, let me explain sumthin' to you. I'm a woman of my word. That's all I have. My girls and I don't play. This is what it is, Tai."

Reesie disconnected the call. Reesie, Mya and Libra arrived at their destination five minutes early. When they enter the parking lot, Taijeon and Sameon were there waiting. Sameon informed them to follow him. Reesie obliged his demand. She knew the cops didn't tolerate any bullshit in U City, one of St. Louis's historical areas.

As they approached North and South Boulevard, Reesie asked Libra and Mya, "I know ya'll strapped. That's the reason we went home first," Reesie stated very seriously.

"C'mon, we gon' go on a mission, not knowin' what the outcome, maybe! I should slap you for askin' that retarded ass question," Mya said laughing.

They all carried a nickel-plated nine-millimeter with the silencer. They followed the twins into a garage with a well-manicured lawn. The house itself was beautiful. Sameon immediately made the transaction from the van to the car. Mya and Libra kept their eyes on Sameon, waiting on him to make the wrong move. He was very observant of them, as well. Reesie and Taijeon made their transaction, also. "I see you and your girls like black," Taijeon said to Reesie.

"Yeah," was all Reesie said to Taijeon, giving him a black Christian Dior bag. "Count yo' money before I leave," Reesie said, sounding impatient.

"You good, St. Louis. I trust you," Taijeon implied, exposing the contents in the bag.

"Taijeon please return my bag the next time we meet?"

And with that said Reesie kept it movin'.

The trio made the $3900 in two days. Reesie was anxious to give Taijeon his money. The party was in two days, and she needed to take care of business soon as possible. She hoped Taijeon could meet her at his home— or better yet, was he in town? Reesie didn't want to travel without her girls. She phoned Taj.

Ring, ring!

"Hey New York," Reesie stated.

"Hey yourself! I didn't expect to hear from you so soon," Taijeon said, sounding surprised.

"I don't wanna toot my own horn, but I'm good," Reesie said confidently.

"How soon you want to see me?"

"Today if possible, are you in town?"

"Yes, St. Louis, I am."

"Good! What's a good time for you?"

"Right now," said Taijeon. "Let's make it the same place and same routine."

"See you in twenty minutes," Reesie said, disconnecting the call.

Reesie called Mya and informed her of the situation. Libra was with Nutcase so they didn't want to bother her. They reached Taijeon's house, and this time, he invited them in.

"Would you ladies like anything to drink?" Taijeon asked, extending his hospitality.

"No, thank you," the ladies said unison.

"Can I please use yo' bathroom?" Mya asked.

"Yeah, it's straight down the hall to your left," Taijeon said to Mya. "I'm impressed, St. Louis. I see ya'll is about business. I'ma let the trees go for eight hundred a pound. Ya'll know that's some fruit."

"That's all good, twin," Mya replied coming from the bathroom. "You're droppin' 'em like they hot. Let me snatch ten of 'em. I have exactly what I need to purchase that amount. You do the calculations, sir."

Reesie gave Taijeon a black Prada bag. He took the money and put it on the money counter machine. The total came to $8000.

Taijeon didn't know the females were about their grind. They had to eat, too.

"St. Louis, I'ma throw five of them trees in there fo' ya'll just on GP. The price remains the same. Make this money, ladies. Don't let it make you," Taijeon said to them.

"Say no more," Reesie stated.

Mya didn't say much. She let Reesie negotiate. They were astonished at Taijeon's generosity.

The Day of the Party

The day of the party, the ladies got the whole nine done. They got their hair done, alone with a manicure and pedicure. They went to the Mac and got a makeover by Kimmie, without the makeup. They shopped at West County Mall, and they had breakfast at Christopher's.

This wasn't any day. It was Libra's birthday, and she was getting the surprise of her life—an alluring surprise at that. Mya and Reesie told Libra they had tickets to the fabulous hair show at the Ambassador. Libra decided on wearing her black Christian Dior pantsuit.

Libra and Nutcase arrived at the Ambassador in style. Nutcase opened the door to his steel blue Bentley for Libra to exit. When she was out of the vehicle, Nutcase kissed her on her full lips.

"Pretty, you look beautiful tonight, and baby, you is sexy as a muthafucka'. Look at what you're doing to me," Nutcase said to Libra while tilting his head down. Libra followed his eyes to see the bulge in the front of his pants.

"Boy, you so crazy," Libra replied, smiling and showing her deep dimples. She knew her dimples turned him on.

"Crazy 'bout you," Nutcase says as he winked his eye at Libra.

"I see Mya and Reesie are already here." Libra had noticed Mya's truck.

"Yeah, I told them to come early. You know, I like promptness," Nutcase stated showing his pearly whites.

The couple entered the Ambassador wearing matching black Christian Dior Trench coats. Their coats were taken, entered in the coat check and admired amongst the employees. Nutcase escorted Libra through two massive double doors.

"Surprise!" everyone said in unison. Libra covered her face astonished at what she saw. She noticed the guests, but the hall was immaculate. The decor was silver and pink. There was an ice structure of a scale with Libra's face weighing the left side down. Her invitation had the same photo. She also had silver and pink balloons in the shape of a scale at every table, which was unique. Sixty-inch plasma televisions were on all four walls. Libra saw herself on all four of them.

The one hundred guests had a choice to order from an expensive handmade menu in the shape of a scale. The pink roses were lovely at each table, accompanied by a bottle of Moet on chill. The cake sat on a table by itself, also in the shape of a scale with Libra's photo on it. The cake was strawberry with pink roses surrounded with strawberry whipped cream from K'nodles, one of St. Louis's finest bakeries. Libra was a little teary-eyed, admiring the extravaganza Nutcase had put together. She knew right then that he would always be a part of her life. He received hugs and kisses the whole night from Libra.

Mya and Reesie hugged Libra. "Happy birthday, Scales!" Reesie said, giving Libra her present, and Mya did the same.

"You bitches knew all along," stated Libra while they were in a group hug.

Mya gave her Chanel earrings, and Reesie gave her a matching necklace.

Libra rocked her black Christian Dior pantsuit with the matching stilettos accommodated with the bag. Her accessories consisted of a platinum Rolex watch with her name engraved on it, all iced out, along with her necklace with a small ten-carat charm of a scale. She also had ten carats in her ears. Nutcase had showered her with those gifts this morning before he sent the trio to pamper themselves.

Nutcase wanted Libra to eat, because he had another major surprise for her. But it was her day! She could have it her way like Burger King. Mrs. Wright and Mr. John were there, also. Mrs. Wright had helped Reesie with the decor.

"Somebody loves that ass," Mrs. Wright said to Libra, giving her a hug.

"I guest you're right, Ma. Hey Mr. John, thanks for comin'."

"Naw, thank you fo' inviting an old man like myself," said Mr. John, hugging Libra.

The party was off the chain. All of Nutcase's friends were there like Slick, and a lot of somebodies from da hood if you were making money. Everybody that was getting some for real money was there. Money was Tyron's m.o. Ol' yeah, he showed out for Libra's birthday. He did the damn thing.

Libra kept her man close. Even though she had this thing for Keke, she knew she'd never find another man like Nutcase. He was looking like a Susan B. Anthony, a whole dollar, fuck a dime. This man had the body of LL Cool J, the voice of Barry White, the mannerism of Denzel Washington, the brain of Master P. Tyron's bank account was large and in charge like Michael Jordan's. He was chocolate and bald-headed like Tyrese, the singer. He was all so fine like Will Smith. He was extremely a black man. Libra had every woman's dream man in the palm of her hands.

Nutcase excused himself. He exited the building but wasn't missed. Upon his arrival he took the stage and retrieved the microphone to propose a toast. "Excuse me everyone! Could I please have your attention? And baby, will you join me on stage please with yo' fine ass?"

Libra obliged her man's request.

"Pretty," Nutcase said to Libra, "I hope you're having a wonderful time. I want to wish you a happy, safe and blessed birthday. Of course, you will! You'll be with me."

Everyone laughed.

"You know this wasn't possible without the help of some special people, Mya, Reesie and Mrs. Wright. Here we have the cook, the decorator and the coordinator. I thank ya'll from the bottom of my heart. Baby, I have one more surprise for you. Come with me," Nutcase said reaching for Libra's hand. They connected hands and he led the way.

On the outside of the colossal doors, Libra couldn't believe her eyes. Nutcase had purchased her a black 2004 Infiniti Truck. It had a big silver bow wrapped around it. The truck was beautiful. The interior was soft white leather. He'd had three televisions installed, one on the dashboard and one in each headrest. The stereo system was custom-made, containing a twenty-disc changer. Tyron had all of Libra's favorite music in the disc changer already. He had all of Mary J. Blige, Jill Scott, Anthony Hamilton, and

Tupac's *All Eyes on Me* and *Me Against the World*; both of
Jahiem, Beyonce; and, of course, straight from the Lou,
Nelly and a few others.

The truck had twenty-four-inch rims with spinners.
The spinners were custom-made with a scale in the center
of the spinners. When the truck was in motion, the spinners
spun but the scale stayed still. The license plates read:
Scales. The truck was pleasing to the eye.

Libra removed her Cartier glasses to wipe her tears.
She walked up to Tyron and kissed him passionately.
"Thank you, Tyron baby. I don't know what to say."

"Just say you're having a good time. That's all the
thanks I need," Nutcase said as he kissed the tears away
from Libra's face.

Everyone on the inside viewed the festivities on the
wall-to-wall plasma televisions. As was acknowledged
before, Libra was every woman's nightmare and every
man's dream.

When Libra finished with her man, her friends-
sisters were waiting for her with crocodile tears rolling
down their faces.

Reesie said to Libra, "Scales this is what it is."

"Naw, Reesie, this is what it's gon' be, ya hear
me?"

"Shit! I hear ya," said Mya.

The ladies embraced and laughed. They joined the
others inside. Libra became aware of a lot of faces she
hadn't seen earlier. All of St. Louis's finest comedians Lil
Sam, St. Louis Slim, Maurice G., Eric Rivers and Arvin
Mitchell all approached her wishing her happy birthday.
Tyron had even invited one of the local radio stations,
100.3 The Beat. Everyone was having a fantastic time.

Libra was enjoying herself until Keke and Pooh
walked in. She couldn't believe her eyes. She had to
remove her Cartier glasses again to make sure she wasn't

hallucinating or had too much to drink. She had to keep her composure in front of Nutcase, because she didn't want him to suspect anything. Libra's panties weren't touching her anywhere, but deep down inside, she was a raging bull.

She thought, *How could he bring this bitch to my party knowing we got static? And to top it off, he and I just took a trip together and made the best fucking love! Ol' no, good funky ass stinky ass dog!*

Nutcase was pleased because he knew Keke had nothing on him. He didn't know how to treat a lady of Libra's caliber. Tyron had personally invited Keke and Pooh.

Libra noticed a familiar face staring at her quite often. She excused herself to the restroom. As she proceeded, she made small talk with different people but kept it movin'. When she got closer she recognized the face. It was the female Nutcase had been talking to at Club 314. Libra entered the restroom and the female entered shortly after. Libra wanted to approach the female but didn't know if she would have to beat her ass for tripping. But fuck it, this was her party and if anybody was going to spoil it, it may as well be her. What else can happen? This ol' bitch ass nigga walked in here with a bitch she got static with? If the bitch gets out of line, she got her best friend with her, that .45.

"Excuse me," Libra said to the woman.

"Yes," the woman replied.

"Do you know me or sumthin'? I noticed you staring at me throughout the night."

"No, I don't, but I've heard a lot about you."

"From whom?" Libra asked, serious.

"Yes, you may. From Baldhead."

"Excuse me!" Libra said knowing exactly to whom she was referring to. "Oh, you mean Tyron," she stated acrimoniously, looking the female up and down.

"Oh, I'm Desha, his first love." She extended her hand to Libra. Libra left her hand hanging. "I'm tryin' to see if you're all that I've heard you are—the one that's keeping Baldhead happy these days. You're his whole conversation."

"Well, Desha, you know my name and I'm his last love and I've heard nothin' about you. And just for the record, I know what to do for my man and how to do it. I don't need other bitches watchin' my man or me. He's very satisfied and I'm willin' to bet *your* life on that." With that said, Libra exited the restroom and kept it movin'.

Libra joined her man and friends. They were on the dance floor, showing out. Libra and Nutcase dirty danced the whole time, and Mya danced with a few of Nutcase's friends. Even Mrs. Wright and Mr. John cut the rug. DJ Toss and Ted were off the chain. Reesie was even having a good time.

Libra and Nutcase left the dance floor and went back to the table. They were in a deep conversation when Libra noticed Desha coming to their table.

"I wanted you all to know that I was leaving and to wish you a happy birthday, Libra. Baldhead, please call me tomorrow so we can discuss the business plans," Desha said, rubbing Nutcase head.

"Tyron what is she talkin' about?" said Libra. "No, Desha, you tell me what you're talkin' about. I don't appreciate you comin' to my table, talkin' to my man, then rubbin' his head in front of me like I'm not fuckin' here. I don't play bitches disrespectin' me. I just told you that in the restroom. I know what to do and how to please my man. So you betta' speed on before you get peed on, bitch! Don't try to play on my intelligence, because I won't allow you to, you nasty trick. Now keep it movin'."

"Who are you calling a nasty trick, Libra? Did you forget that you're the one that's fucking Keke? Now, who's the nasty bitch?" Desha said as she looked at Libra with her hands on her hips. "See Tyron, I told you this bitch wasn't about shit. She a gold digging hoe like all the rest of them. I'm the only one that really ever loved you and always will."

Nutcase was astonished and didn't say anything until he saw Libra reach for her pistol.

"Bitch, if you wanna see tomorrow you betta' keep it movin like I educated you the first time," he said

Desha turned to walk away but before she left she asked Nutcase, "Are you going to be with this bitch and you know she's cheating on you? You are a fool in love. When love starts making you act like a fool, it's time to leave love alone," Desha barked to Nutcase.

Before Desha could blink her eyes Libra popped her in the nose with the butt of her pistol. Libra looked at Nutcase to see his reaction but didn't really give a fuck, because she felt Desha was out of order. Nutcase grabbed Libra and took her outside.

"Tyron let me the fuck go. If you thought I was cheating on you, all you had to do was ask me. You didn't have to confide in another bitch. Yo' ex bitch at that! Damn Tyron!" Libra said dropping her hands, very unhappy with Nutcase.

"Baby, it wasn't like that. Look can we just leave and talk and enjoy the rest of your birthday and the other surprise I have for you?"

Desha was escorted to her car by the security guards as Libra and Nutcase walked back in to retrieve their coats.

Deesha shouted, "Bitch, I got you. Every time you close your muthafuckin' eyes, you're going to have nightmares about me! Baldhead, you better tell that bitch who I am."

Libra pulled away from Nutcase, got in Desha's face and looked her in her eyes. "Little girl, let me explain sumthin' to you. I don't have nightmares 'cause I don't fuckin' dream. And if you don't get the fuck away from here, murder will be the case they gave me. You better ask Snoop Dog b-it-ch," Libra said. As she turned to walk away she spit in Desha's face.

Desha broke loose from the guard and ran Libra's way, but before she made it, Libra pointed her pistol at Desha's face.

"C'mon bitch! Make my muthafuckin' day, would you please?"

At this point, everybody was exiting the hall. Mya and Reesie came running to Libra, followed by Mrs. Wright and Mr. John.

"Scales, what's good?" asked Reesie.

"Bitch wanna act up and got smacked up, that's all. I hope her fuckin' nose is broke. I'm good. The situation has been dealt wit'."

"That's right, Libra baby," stated Mrs. Wright. "Don't you never ever let a bitch disrespect you. You always stand up and demand your respect. I always told you girls that when you all were growing up."

Mya was mad at hell. She didn't say much. Nutcase wanted to get Libra away from there and calm her down, but he knew that was going to be tough with her girls around.

"Baby, let's go. I got a reservation at Chase Park Plaza. We can talk when we get there."

"I'm ready. Let's go. But first let me say my goodbyes."

Libra walked back into the hall, announced that she was leaving and thanked everybody for coming. She talked to Mya and Reesie for a second. She gave Keke the dirtiest look, grabbed Nutcase's arm and kept it movin'

Chapter 11

Let the Truth Be Told

Libra and Nutcase reached the Chase Park Plaza on Kingshighway Boulevard and Lindell Boulevard. There wasn't too much conversation on the way there. Once they reached the room, Libra went to take a bath. She was so pissed; she didn't noticed how beautiful the room was. While she was in the bathtub, Nutcase came in and joined her. She didn't say anything but made room for him.

"Tyron, is there sumthin' you wanna ask me? Because if there is, then do so, 'cause I don't appreciate yo' lil girlfriend all up in my buz'ness, puttin' it in the streets like she did. You wouldn't happen to know anythin' 'bout that, would you?" Libra asked Nutcase nastily.

"Yes, it's a couple of things I want to inquire about when it comes to Keke. I know ya'll had a thing going, but I thought it was long over with. I was in the office the day after you left for your trip when I got a phone call informing me that my lady was with another man, and you know who that man was? Keke." Libra couldn't say anything, because she knew it was true. "I never asked you because I didn't see it, but I knew the information was correct."

"How do you know that?" asked Libra, running more hot water in the tub.

"That's neither here nor there. I want to know, is there something going on between you and Keke? And Libra, please don't lie to me. Tell the truth, shame the devil."

The way Nutcase looked at Libra, she knew she had to tell him the truth, because he wasn't having it any other way.

Libra looked at Nutcase and said, "I will not lie to you because I owe you that much, and if it's the truth you want, the truth you'll get. Tyron, it was over between Keke and me before it started."

"Libra, what I want to know is did Keke go out of town with you, and did you fuck him? All that other shit is irrelevant. This is a yes or no question."

Libra knew Nutcase was a no-nonsense type of nigga, and deep inside, she knew she couldn't lie to him because he knew the answer. She also feared what he might do to her, but this was a chance she would have to take.

"Tyron, the answer to all your questions is yes. I can't explain why things happened the way they did, but they did. I don't wanna lose you, but if you decide to end our relationship, I will understand. I never meant to hurt you in anyway, because you've been nothin' but good to me."

The water was getting cold and Nutcase took his time responding to Libra. She didn't know what to do or think. He just stared at Libra shaking his head.

"Baby, say sumthin'. Just don't keep staring at me."

"Damn Libra I wanted to think it was a lie, but I had a gut feeling the information was correct. If I was doing something that wasn't pleasing to you, you could have told me."

Nutcase never once raised his voice, but Libra could tell he was very upset, although he kept his composure.

"Tyron, what will happen wit' us?" Libra asked in a low tone.

"What the fuck you think will happen with us? Libra, you cheated on me, and I've never thought about being with anyone but you. I gave you my heart. I know I

102

had to love you because we were raw dogging it. I could
never trust you again, and I can't be with any one that I
can't trust, so this shit is finished. You can keep that shit I
got you for your birthday, that's nothing to me. Desha kept
telling me you weren't shit, but my stupid ass was in love
and couldn't see the light. You had me walking around here
with an F stamped on my forehead, and she was right.
When love starts making you act like a fool, its time to
leave love the fuck alone, and that's what I'm about to do."

Nutcase removed himself from the tub and said to
Libra, "I will call you a cab, because I have nothing else to
say to you."

"Tyron, you're goin' to give up on us just like
that?" Libra asked with tears rolling down her face.

"Yes, just like that. Shit you did. Libra you are a
flagrant bitch, and let me get the fuck away from you,
because I'm not held responsible for what I might do to you
if I continue to be in the same room with you."

Nutcase got out of the tub, wrapped the Polo towel
around him, walked out the bathroom and started putting on
his clothes. Libra sat in the tub and cried like a baby,
because at that very moment, she realized how much she
cared for Nutcase, and losing him for Keke was not in her
plans. She had never heard Nutcase disrespect her the way
he did at that moment and her feelings were shadowed.

Libra pulled herself together and got out the tub to
call Mya to come and get her. "Tyron, I don't need a cab.
Mya's comin' to get me."

He never said a word or looked her way. He kept
reading the *Evening Whirl*, one of St. Louis's newspapers,
the ghetto version of the *Post Dispatch*. Libra continued to
get dressed, and before she knew it, Mya was calling her
cell phone, letting her know she was in the lobby. When
Libra grabbed her purse to leave, Nutcase stopped her.

"Ms. Love, can I ask you a question just for the record?"

Libra nodded her head "yes."

"Did you strap up with that nigga? Tell me you did."

"I did, Tyron," Libra said, walking out the door with tears in her eyes.

Nutcase felt like a part of him had died, but he wouldn't be anyone's fool. He thought about all the pussy women threw at him. His pussy rate was large, but Libra was his heart. He felt like he didn't want to be alone, so he called and checked on Desha and she ended up in the hotel room with him, in the bed that was supposed to be for him and Libra. At that very second, he promised himself that he would never give his heart to anyone else.

Crying, Libra entered the car with Mya and Reesie. She didn't know Reesie was coming, and the support was needed.

"Scales what's wrong?" asked Mya.

"Everythin'!" She busted in tears. "It's over with Tyron and me. He knows about Keke and me. I lost the best thing in my life that ever happened to me, and for what! Some dick!"

She was crying uncontrollably at this point.

"You see, Scales, I told you that you had a good man and to think about the choices you make. You know Mama always told us we make our beds so we have to lay in it," Reesie stated unsympathetically.

"Res, don't nobody wanna hear that shit at a time like this. The damn girl's hurting," said Mya, giving Libra a tissue.

"Mya, why should I have to sugar coat the situation? When shit was goin' down wit' Caelin and me, did you sugar coat it? Fuck no! So what makes Scales any different? I'm not sayin' this to hurt her. I'm tryin' to help her. Regardless of what happens, I'm here for you. We're Derrty E N T baby. We all we got. You're my sistah, girl. Remember those words, Scales?"

Reesie reassured her by wiping the tears from her eyes with the tissue.

"She's right, Mya. I let her have it when she was goin' through wit' Caelin to make her stronger, so I guess one favor deserves another one, right? I guess what don't kill you can only make you stronger. That's what they say."

"I'm never goin' to say nor do anythin' to hurt you, believe that," said Reesie. "But keepin' it real, that's the only way I can let you have it. And Mya, you shut the fuck up and find you a man of yo' own, bitch."

"That was cold, Res," stated Libra, but they all laughed about it.

Chapter 12

When It Rains, It Pours

A month had passed since Libra and Nutcase had broken up. She still hadn't spoken to him. She missed him tremendously. She tried calling, but he had changed all of his numbers except his two-way pager. She emailed him but got no return message. She even decided to go by his house, but before she parked, she saw him kissing Desha. She parked behind his Denali truck so she couldn't be seen. She put her head on the steering wheel and cried uncontrollably, not realizing she was leaning on the horn.

Nutcase hadn't made it into the house yet and noticed the 300. He walked over to the car and knocked on the window. The knock scared the shit out of Libra. She jumped as she looked up. He motioned for her to let the window down. Libra obliged his request.

"What are you doing coming to my house unannounced?" Tyron asked in a not-so-pleasant tone. Libra said nothing but continued to let the tears flow. "I would appreciate it if you would call before you make an appearance."

"I emailed you but you didn't return the message," Libra explained sadly.

"Then that should have told you something. Libra, we didn't end our relationship because we didn't agree on something. You cheated on me, and I can't forget about that. Maybe forgive, but never forget."

"Nutcase, I know I made a mistake, a damn full-size mistake, but I'm only human. If you care about me the way you claim you do, then givin' me another chance shouldn't be an issue."

"Libra please let that be the reason. You knew how much I cared about you. What you want me to do, write it on the Good Year Blimp. Will you just leave? I don't feel like having this discussion anymore. Things will remain the same. If I can't trust you, then I don't need you. It's as simple as that. Have a good day."

Nutcase walked away from the car, never looking back. Libra sat there until he was out of sight, wondering if he had given up on her that effortlessly. As she got ready to pull off, she saw a silver Maxima 2.5S pull up on the side.

"Bitch, I told you he was mine. You don't know what to do with a man like Tyron, so keep fucking with them ghetto ass niggas. Libra let me warn you honey, you can take the girl out the ghetto, but you can't take the ghetto out the girl. Catch my drift?" confirmed Desha with a smirk on her face, winking her eye at Libra.

"Well Desha, let me tell you sumthin', Ms. Know-It-All. As I acknowledged before, you don't know a damn thing about me. I don't have to explain myself. Who the fuck you think you are, God or some muthafuckin body?"

As Libra spoke to Desha, she exited her car and walked around to Desha's car and pulled her out. Desha didn't see it coming. Libra grabbed her by her hair through the window of her car and she hits the ground. Nutcase was looking out of his window and saw the incident. He came running to save Desha again, but this time Libra slapped him in the face.

"I know you're not siding wit' this bitch, Tyron. You know what, I'm through! You can have her. Fuck you and this bullshit. Desha, hoe, you better stay the fuck outta my way before I commit murder. And bitch, you're not worth my freedom.

"Tyron, when this bitch fucks over you, don't think I'm goin' to be there waitin', 'cause I'm not. You think I hurt you? This the type of hoe you gotta keep an eye on, not me. I keeps it real. They don't come real as me, Boo Boo."

"Then Libra, that's a chance I'm going to take."

Tryon grabbed Desha by her waist and they walked into the house. At that very moment Libra realized that she was done with this situation. She had thought if she was a woman about what she did and told Nutcase the truth, he would honor her more, but instead, she lost him completely.

Getting back in her car she thought, *We win some and we loose some. Ol' muthafuckin well, he lost this one.*

She played Juvenile CD, Juvy the Great. She selected *Bounce Back* and blasted it to the max and kept it movin'.

Chapter 13

Mrs. Marquita Wright

Mrs. Marquita Wright was one of the coolest people you will ever meet in your life. She had a reputation for taking no shit. Mrs. Wright didn't give a fuck about nothing but her girls, Reesie, Libra and Mya. Reesie was her biological daughter. Libra and Mya were daughters she did not give birth to, but it was either hell or jail for all three of them. She had custody of Libra and Mya since they were nine years old. Back in her younger days, she was nothing nice. Growing up, she had two best friends, also. They were taken away from her in a hideous crime, but they had made a promise to each other and she kept her end of the bargain. They all agreed if something happened to any of them, they would take care of each other's children. They never thought that they would depart at the same time.

Mya's mother, Mia, was a lot like her daughter, very promiscuous and loose. She was the hot commodity back in the day. The men loved her chocolate complexion and big booty. If they wanted Mia, they had to pay for every inch of her body, and she didn't mind selling it if the price was right.

Linda, on the other hand, was in a class by herself. She had an angel face like her daughter and very profound dimples as well. Her hair hung down the center of her back. Linda knew her friends were untamed at times, and she knew with her around, they could be stopped from doing some preposterous things.

Linda and Libra's father were on bad terms, and Mia wanted her to get out and get Curtis off her mind. Linda agreed to double date with Mia and her friend.

Neither one of the ladies know how treacherous these guys were. Mia would do anything to have a good time, and Linda wasn't down with that. The guys wanted them to shoot heroin in their arms, and Linda disagreed. Linda's date became extremely angry.

"This bitch thinks she's too good to hang with us. Man, I told you 'bout settin' me up wit' those goin' to church on Sunday hoes. I can't touch this bitch or nothin'."

"Joe, you can hold all of that down, muthafucka? Don't you eva' disrespect my sistah again! That's why you can't get a for real woman, 'cause you don't know how to treat them. You should know class when you see it like CR.

"That's right, Joe, treat the lady with respect."

"Fuck that! I want some of this sweet pussy, and she's gonna give it to me."

He pulled Linda by her long hair, which she had in a pony tail, and roughly yanked her head. Linda removed a knife in her purse and put it in her bra when she saw how violent he was. CR knew what the plan was. He had fallen in love with Mia. He knew about all the men she ran around with and wanted to make her pay for that. Even though CR had a wife and kid at home, he wanted to have his cake and eat it too, and some ice cream on top as well..

CR didn't know if Joe was going along with the plan or if the dope had taken control over him that quickly, but whatever the situation was, he didn't think it would get out of hand like it did. But he had to roll with the program. Mia became upset when she heard Linda screaming. She was in the room with CR, shooting up. She tried to rescue Linda when CR grabbed her by the throat and choked her. Linda reached for the knife she had in her bra and cut Joe's leg. The cut was superficial. That just made him more annoyed. That's when he shot her in the head with a .38 special. When he finished with Linda, he gave the gun to

CR and he did the same thing to Mia. They left Linda and Mia's bodies in a vacant building on the east side.

Their bodies had been missing for weeks. Some worker was gutting a building out when the gruesome bodies were discovered. When they walked in, the odor was the first thing that hit them. The news traveled quickly. Mrs. Wright had reported the women missing within a twenty-four-hour period. She knew in her heart that something wasn't right. Curtis accused Mrs. Wright of hiding Linda from him. But when he saw his daughter asking for her mother, he knew she wasn't lying about her whereabouts.

Mrs. Wright made a promise to herself that she would find the lowdown, dirty, funky, no good for nothing niggas that did this to her sister-friends. She also knew that she had to keep her promise that they had made to each other if something happened to any one of them. She knew she was going to have to deal with Curtis about his little girl, but that was a battle she was willing to fight if need be.

The hardest part of all this was telling young Libra and Mya that they would never see their mothers again except when they lay in their coffins. At that time, Mrs. Wright dealt with nothing but hard-core niggas, and they did anything she wanted them to do. Word got out on the streets that there was a million-dollar reward for the killer or killers of her sisters-friends, and the streets started talking. The only person that was captured was Joe. CR had left the country for a while.

Mrs. Wright found Joe on the east side at a strip club called The Pink Slip. Dirty Red, an old school pimp, player, and hustler accompanied her. Dirty Red was the nigga back in the day, like Jigga, Hova or Jay-Z. Mrs. Wright had gigantic hips and a small waist, which she passed to her daughter. Old and young guys craved for Mrs. Wright. If your financial status equaled Quincy Jones', you had a soldier on your team. She had Dirty Red's nose wide open, and anything could go down. He parked his red Cadillac in front of the establishment.

He walked Mrs. Wright to the VIP area. Their drinks were waiting for them. Mrs. Wright heard that this was Joe's hangout so she stayed on her p's&q's looking for this lowdown muthafucka.'She made sure she did not drink too much. "Never drunk, just drank" was her motto.

Mrs. Wright paid attention to everything that went on around her. She was a true ear hustler. Dirty Red received seductive looks, angry looks and even envious looks, but they knew not to get out of control or it would cost them their life. Mrs. Wright waited and waited but Joe had not shown up. She even looked at the fellows that were getting lap dances. Still no Joe. She searched every table, observing everything in the club. Still no Joe. She went so far as to peek in the men's bathroom. After no Joe, she gave up on seeing him that night.

One of the waitresses named Jasmine walked over to Dirty Red. "Is everything all right over here, people?" she asked very sociably.

"Yes, thank you," replied Mrs. Wright, thinking this was the most unattractive female she had ever seen in her life.

"Everything is everything, Jasmine." Dirty Red said as he read the newspaper.

"Dirty Red, can I ask you a question?" asked Mrs. Wright with a slight smile on the face.

"Yes," he said sternly.

"Where did you get that drag queen from? She looks just like a man?"

"Shit baby, I don't do the hiring. Nasty man Mark does. You know he's old and anything looks good to him," he said, continuing to read the paper.

"Well, I hope she don't live off this salary, because I know she's evicted. Who pays for something like that?"

"Baby, you would be surprised at what these men pay for these days."

Mrs. Wright forgot about Joe and continued to have a good time with Dirty Red. She also eye witnessed that Jasmine indeed had a lot of fans. Chills went through her body, because this was an unsightly woman. Mrs. Wright looked at the woman once more and discovered that it was Joe!

"Dirty Red, you think my brother will have a good time with her?"

"It depends on what your brother likes, baby. If he likes ladies, then no, but if he likes trash he will have a good time."

"One man's trash is another man's treasure, sweetie," Mrs. Wright stated, laughing at this point. "I'll tell him, and he can come see for himself."

They had a little more conversation and the night ended for them. They have always kept in touch: You know, girls, have you ever had a friend that you get with every now and then? That was Mrs. Wright's relationship with Dirty Red.

One week later, Mrs. Wright sent her play brother over there to confirm what she already knew. JR was sitting there, talking to Jasmine before the club closed and JR invited her to go with him.

"Hey sugar!" JR flagged her down with a stack of bills in his hand.

"Yes, can I help you, sir?" Jasmine stated, again very pleasantly.

"Keep the R&R coming?"

"Sure will, sir. Anything else?"

"Yes. You! After work."

"Excuse me," Jasmine said, unsure of what she had heard.

"Did I offend you? If so, I'm so very sorry," stated JR pleasurably.

"Not at all. That was extremely nice of you," Jasmine said, smiling from ear to ear.

JR got Jasmine to come to his house that night. Everything was going accordingly to plan. The basement was really homely and comfortable. Jasmine made herself at home the minute she walked through the door. Little did Jasmine know, Mrs. Wright knew she smoked those sticks. She had them waiting along with something Jasmine could never expect.

She looked around and spotted them like radars. Her antennas went up.

"Baby, make yo'self at home. Go 'head! Fire up one."

JR acknowledged the anxiousness in Jasmine's behavior. But like a rabbit, she hopped out there. He seen the effect the dope had on Jasmine and gave her something she would never expect. JR fired up a joint. Jasmine was so high that she never even paid attention to him giving her the sticks as freely as she requested. The very last one was laced with rat poison, PCP and powdered cocaine mixed together. Jasmine would lose her damn mind fucking with that Killer, as they called it back in the day.

Jasmine saw things she knew didn't exist until she smoked that Killer. She thought she had seen an elephant and lion fighting in the basement. JR entertained her while Mrs. Wright saved the best for last. Jasmine was dreadfully paranoid. She thought she was losing her mind.

"Hi Joe," said Mrs. Wright, seductively.

"My fuckin' name ain't Joe. I'm Jasmine. Can't you see that?" she said, screaming and yelling hysterically out of control. Mrs. Wright shot her in the right foot with her

.357 with a potato stuck on the end acting as a silencer. Jasmine quieted down a notch.

"Joe, I want you to know I know what you did to my sistahs, you and the punk ass bitch CR. I can't end your life just by killing you, nigga. You have to suffer. You took away the people that meant the most to me in this world. You know what they said?"

"Naw Marquita. What they say?" Joe asked dryly.

"Nigga, don't insult my intelligence. When you lie down with a dog, you get up with fleas, you rapist."

One shot to the other foot. Joe was feeling more of the pain now than before.

"That bitch though she was too good," Joe whispered in more excruciating pain. Mrs. Wright ended the activities for the night. She wanted Joe-Jasmine to sleep the high down and torment him more when he would be in a more sober state of mind..

"Why you gotta hold grudges against a nigga, Marquita? I didn't have nothin' to do wit' those killings. CR is a cold-hearted nigga. You know he made a nigga do dirt 'cuz I was weak. You know, a pussy, as you call it."

"Pussy! That's what I still call it. Tell me, what's changed? I'm still that same bitch that will put a cap in that ass. Now tell me where that poor excuse of a man CR is. It might spare yo' life, pussy. You wanna call yourself an OG, nigga, but you get down like you Rapaul. And just for the record, you shole is ugly," laughed Mrs. Wright, one shot in each kneecap.

"Girl, you know how CR skips town. Ain't no tellin' where he at." Joe said with excruciating pain. Don't hold me responsible for what CR made me do."

Joe was showing that he was afraid of what Mrs. Wright might do, and he had every reason to be.

"Joe, I'm tired of playing with you, so take this death-like a whippin'. Only it's no coming back from death."

First she sprayed bleach in his wounds then she made him open his mouth and shot him in his throat. "JR, clean this mess up please. That other pussy got his comin'. Trust and believe."

Mrs. Wright was a woman of her word. And with that said, she kept it movin and felt no remorse. Why should she? He didn't feel any for her sistahs-friends.

Marquita Wright was pleased that she had found Joe, but she wanted to be satisfied, and only killing CR would fulfill that desire. From that day on, she continued her search.

Chapter 14

Facing Reality

Libra realized that it was over with her and Nutcase. She'd tried to mend the situation, but she felt he was acting like a little bitch. The incident would no longer bother her. At this point, she would only focus on making money. Libra also felt that she would get over him with the help of her girls. She reached her house and found Reesie's truck parked in the driveway but did not see Mya's truck. She assumed they were together until she heard *Love of My Life* blasting from the speakers.

"Scales, you look like shit. What happen to you?"

Libra looked at Reesie and shook her head as if to say, *You don't wanna know.*

"I made a damn fool of myself."

"How you do that?" Reesie looked alarm.

"I went over to Tyron's house and had to spank Desha's ass. The bitch thinks I'ma joke. I went to talk to my man, but from the look of things, he's not my man anymore."

Libra held her head down as she gave Reesie the details. Her feelings were wrecked.

"Scales, I hate to be the bearer of bad news, but you knew that before you went over there."

"Yeah, I know, but I thought if I gave him a little time, we could talk about it later. But like he said, he can forgive but he can't forget. Oh well."

"We learn from our mistakes. Dust yo'self off and try again, you know," Reesie said.

She walked over to Libra and gave her a hug. They laughed. "You're my sistah, girl."

"I know," Libra stated in better spirits.

"Res, what's up wit' Taijeon? I know he's pleased wit' the work."

"We don't have any complaints from him at all. He's very flirtatious. I told him I don't mix buz'ness with pleasure. He is cute though."

"Bitch, you sneaky. Tell the truth and shame the devil, you like him don't cha?"

"No, I really don't. I was tryin' to make this money, that all. Scales, I'm really thinkin' about quittin'. It's not like we need the money. All three of us are okay. What you think?"

"Reesie, if that's what you wanna do, it's cool wit' me. The only thin' that matters is yo' happiness. It doesn't matter to me one way or the other."

"I'm glad you're okay wit' that, but now I gotta holla at Mya, see what she thinks. Dig, Scales, she has been missin' in action lately. What's that hoe up to?" Reesie asked, rocking to the music.

"You know she got a new piece of dick, that's all. Speaking of dick, what's up wit' you and Caelin?"

"Not a muthafuckin' thin'. I wanna go get some of my things, but I'm try'na wait til he's gone. I called him the other day to see where he was and he wanted me to come to the house, but I'm not as crazy as I may act sometimes. He wasn't whippin' my ass. Will you go wit' me when I go?"

You could detect the gloom in Reesie's voice as she spoke.

"Fo' sho'. You're my sistah girl. What kind of question is that? I told you we're in this together. Res, I learned some details about Mya I'm not pleased wit', and I hope they are not true," Libra said on a more serious note.

"What, Scales? Don't leave me in the dark. I've already heard, but I wanted to check it out first. I was thinkin' about hiring a private detective, and once everythin' checked out I was gonna confirm it wit' you."

"We don't have to hire no PI. Officer Brown will do anythin' for a piece of pussy. I'ma holla at him. He's about his work. I'll give him three grand to think about it. You know that fat muthafucka' is about the almighty dollar, wit' his big ass," Libra assured Reesie.

"Scales have him to run a check on Taijeon and Sameon as well. I know he been more than good to us, but he's up to sumthin' and I'm not for no bullshit. Get on that now, please! Don't go in the room and start thinkin' about Nutcase. This is more important. I'm about to roll out. I'll give you a call later. Check Mya out when she comes in the house. Pay attention to how she's actin'. Holla back."

With that said, Reesie gave Libra a hug and kept it movin'.

Libra went in her room to check her email. She wasn't looking for anything in particular, but to her astonishment, Nutcase had left her a message. The email read: *It's over.*

Libra, don't try to contact me anymore. You have proved to me that you are nothing more than a ghetto bitch, and I disassociate myself from problems and people with problems. What we had is over. I am going to be with Desha, because she demonstrates trustworthiness to me. I can't say that much for you. So do us both a favor and travel on with your life, because this chapter is closed.

After retrieving the message, Libra was dismayed. "I can't believe this pussy foot muthafucka'. I already came to that conclusion when I left his house tonight."

She emailed back:

Already let go, Sweetie. When I left yo' house tonight, that's where I left every memory we shared. So don't flatter yo'self, because it was a time when I didn't know you. And that's how I feel now. Picture this ghetto bitch rollin', nigga!

Libra was too out done by the email, but she kept it movin' and called Officer Brown. He agreed to meet her at nine o'clock the following morning.

Chapter 15

I Want Out

Reesie was meeting with Taijeon later in the week. She was waiting before she made the actual date because she hadn't spoken to Mya yet. She called the house several times a day to contact her, but no luck! Mya had been staying away from home a lot more these days than in the past. Libra and Reesie felt something was awfully wrong because they always called home if they were staying out the entire night. That was so unlike Mya. Reesie felt that if she didn't speak with Mya by the end of the week, this evaluation would be made without her, and that's exactly what happened.

Reesie spoke with Libra and informed her on what was going down. Libra asked Reesie if she wanted her to go with her, and Reesie insisted that she not go. That didn't sit well with Libra. She felt that they were in this together, but she respected her request and did as instructed.

When Libra spoke with Officer Brown, he told her that he would contact her by the end of the week. Libra looked forward to hearing from him. She didn't wait on Officer Brown to call her—she called him. He invited her to his office for the results. In the meantime, Reesie was having her meeting with Taijeon.

Taijeon was not tolerant of the news.

"Look, Taijeon, this shit ain't for me and my girls anymore. We've all decided this is best for us. We thank you for showin' us much love, but everythin' comes to an end." Reesie's tone of voice beamed with poise. She didn't back down. That's one thing Mrs. Wright had taught the girls—never back down on what you accept as true.

Taijeon made an offer that was music to Reesie's ears, but she stuck to her guns. Taijeon was so persistent that she told him she would have to consult with her home girls and get back to him later. To her relief he agreed.

"Reesie I don't like to start a big business association with a person and then they suspend themselves from me. That don't sit well with my kindness. You have one week to determine your decision, and I anticipate that you will make the right choice to the advantage of us all."

"Taijeon, you sound like you're threatening me." Reesie's attitude was real shitty at this point.

"You can call it what you want, St. Louis. I thought I gave you a pretty good deal, and I'm never this generous. They say never trust a big butt and a smile."

Reesie felt something wasn't right with Taijeon, but she disregarded her gut feeling. Mrs. Wright had always told her to follow her first mind and she could never go wrong.

Back at Officer Brown's office, Libra found out things she didn't want to know. He told Libra that Mya was seeing some fellas from New York and she was getting high. Mya was using heroin and coke, and the guy was her supplier. When he showed Libra the pictures, it took everything she had not to fall out of the chair she was sitting in.

"What's wrong, Ms. Love?" Office Brown asked.

"I know this guy. This is Sameon. He has a twin brother name Taijeon, and they are from New York—you know, the guys I asked you to check out for me. We met them when we were out of town for my birthday. What can you tell me about these two?"

Libra's face and voice showed great concern.

"Libra if I may call you that?" Officer Brown confirmed.

"That's fine," she approved.

"I need a little more time with this case. What I do know is these guys are nothing nice. Just give me three days and I will have all the statistics you need."

"You don't understand. I don't have three days," Libra said with annoyance.

"That's the only way I can help you, Ms. Love."

"Three days–nothin' more! I need this information as soon as possible."

"You will hear from me. You got my word, Libra. Don't worry. I will come through for you, okay?" Officer Brown said to Libra with arched eyebrows.

"Thank you so much," Libra said as she shook his hand and left his office.

Chapter 16

More Drama

Libra couldn't believe her ears. She knew something was wrong, but not this. She thought Mya had got dick-happy and decided not to call, not that she was on drugs and with the twins. She always said there was something about those brothers that she didn't like, but she trusted her sister's judgment. Riding in her Infiniti truck, she called Reesie and told her to meet her at the house in twenty minutes. As always, Reesie was there like clockwork.

On her way home, she said a prayer for Mya. "Lord Jesus, if you're listening to me, please watch over Mya. Lord, keep her safe from any destruction that may come her way. Father God, again, you say we have not because we ask not. Lord, I'm askin' in your name, in Jesus' name. Amen."

When Libra made it to the house, Reesie was there. Libra could tell that Reesie had something of her own that she wanted to share. Reesie was playing Anthony Hamilton's CD when Libra entered the house.

"Scales, what's the deal? What you find out?" Reesie asked nervously.

"Res, sit down for this and braces yo'self." Libra gave Reesie the pictures that she had received from Officer Brown. What Reesie saw made her very heated.

"I don't believe this shit!" Reesie said, throwing the pictures across the room. "How could she be so weak-minded. This muthafucka' nigga had to do sumthin' to Mya for her to fuck wit' that shit. She don't get down like that."

Mya was in the van that Sameon and Taijeon had met them in, sucking both of their dicks. There was another picture of her using the dope. That's the one that brought tears to Reesie's eyes. Reesie didn't trip off the one where she was sucking their dicks, because she knew Mya was a freak and got down like she lived.

"Scales, did he tell you where he captured these photos at?" Reesie asked as she wiped the tears from her eyes. "That snake didn't say anythin' about ya'll, 'cause he knew they had Mya. He made it like it was so hard for him to accept that we wanted out."

"Yeah, he said that she's stayin' at their house in University City, but the pictures were taken in Heman Park."

"Scales, are you gonna be cool stayin' here by yo'self tonight? I got some thinkin' to do, and I need to call Lorenzo, 'cause we need his help."

"Res, I'm cool wit' stayin' at home by myself. I'm a big girl. Did you forget? But I'm not cool wit' the fact of Keke being involved wit' our problems."

"Right now it's not about Keke. It's about Mya. Scales, you know if Lorenzo gets involved, it's gonna involve Keke. C'mon now, be reasonable," Reesie stated to Libra with sincerity in her eyes.

"All right, Res, only because ya'll my sistah, girl, and them niggas do know how to find out info, and Lo's a'ight wit' me," Libra said with a smile on her face, showing her deep dimples. The girls hugged and Reesie kept it movin.

Reesie had gone to Caelin's and her house a couple of days later and retrieved her Rodeo truck. She called Lorenzo on his cell phone and told him the 411. He listened carefully and had Reesie meet him at The Best Steak House on North Grand to discuss the plans. As Reesie continued her journey, she noticed a white Mazda 626 following her.

She thought she was tripping, so she paid it no mind. Just so she would feel safe, she put her silver .22 on her lap. She had DMX playing in her CD player. *I'm slippin', I'm fallin', I can't get up.* Reesie sang along with the song and at that moment that was how she felt.

Lorenzo finally made it to the restaurant and they placed their order. Reesie went over the facts again and showed him the photos. He was flabbergasted, and he instantaneously said he would help. They made their plan together and promised to contact each other the next day.

Reesie decided to take a ride to U City to see what was really good. Again, she saw the white Mazda 626 following her. She came to a stoplight and didn't see the car any longer. She felt safe and suddenly out of nowhere, she saw a nine-millimeter pointed at her through her window.

"Bitch get outta the car befo' I blow yo' muthafuckin' brains out."

Reesie didn't know whether to put the medal to the paddle or do as she was told.

"Don't even think about it or yo' mama will be wearin' that black dress, you sorry ass hoe."

Reesie didn't have to open the door. Caelin had his own key. He pulled her by her hair and made her get in his car.

"Ya thought you could get away from me huh?" He slapped Reesie across the face. "Reesie I love ya, and ya think another nigga gon' have ya. Fuck naw! I made ya what ya are, and ya think ya can leave me? Bitch, ya outta yo' eva'lastin' mind. If I can't have ya, no one will. Do ya comprehend that? I told yo' dumb ass that befo', Reesie. What part of that ya don't understand?"

Caelin could make you go crawl under a rock if your self esteem was low. And Reesie wished she was invisible at this time. He had her terrified as hell, and she didn't want to do anything that would activate his fury more. She thought she would play it cool.

"Lay baby, you can get that gun outta my face. You have me now. Where am I going?" Reesie said trying to remain cool.

"Bitch, shut the fuck up. Ya try to be so hip, but I got ya. I told ya I didn't want ya around them haters, but ya said fuck me and did what ya wanted to do, like I'm a pussy or sumthin'."

Reesie could see the fire in Caelin's eyes. And that was not a good thing.

"Caelin, where are you taking me?"

"Don't ask me no questions, bitch. I don't wanna hear yo' voice. It makes me sick to imagine ya wit' that nigga Lorenzo. I can throw up in yo' face."

"Caelin, I'm tellin' you, nothin' is goin' on between Lo and me."

"Res, why ya'll was together tonight, then? Answer that."

Caelin pulled the car to the side of the road just to hear her answer.

"Caelin, Mya's been missin' for some days, now, and we, Libra and I, are tryin' to locate her. That's all, Boo." Reesie said sounding so sincere.

"Res, let me put a bug in yo' ear. It don't matter who's missin', 'cause ya gon' be missin' yo' damn self. You better anticipate on not seein' tomorrow 'cuz ya tried to leave me. Ya thought I wouldn't find ya, but ya were wrong, slut. So ya might as well get comfortable, because ya not goin' nowhere."

Caelin spoke to Reesie like she was the enemy. She knew he was the enemy. She was sleeping with the enemy.

Reesie rode with Caelin for hours, listening to him bitch at her about what she did and didn't do. For the life of her, she didn't know why she'd gotten with him in the first place. But when she met him, he was everything she wanted in a man and more, but that shortly changed when he started spankin' that ass. Before long, they ended up on the Riverfront and Reesie was scared shitless. She didn't know if this disturbed person was going to kill her and throw her in the river. She needed Libra to say a prayer for her at that very instant, because she never prayed. But she did this day.

"Reesie Wright, look at me!" Reesie did as she was told. "Do ya know how much I love ya? Didn't I tell ya if I couldn't have ya no one would?" Caelin said reaching for his gun.

"Yes, you said that Caelin." Reesie's voice trembled as she said those words.

"Did ya think I was lying?" Caelin said putting the gun up to her head.

"No, I didn't Caelin," Reesie said with tears streaming down her face.

"Bitch, ya not so bad now, are ya? When ya went out of town wit' that nigga, ya weren't crying, so don't cry now, Billy bad ass." And Caelin pulled the trigger.

Chapter 17

Blood Thicker Than Water

Caelin continued to ride around. "Ms. Wright, is ya hungry?" Caelin never received an answer. "Don't let me have to ask ya again, Reesie," his voice was stern.

"Yes I'm hungry Caelin." Reesie uttered snobbish.

"What do ya wanna eat? We're goin' pass Jack in the Crack. Ya know ya like those monster tacos. Or we can go to Uncle Bill's on the dirty south. It's all about ya, Boo."

Caelin stated as he pinched Reesie jaw. She moved away from him.

This muthafucka' damn near shoots me, and he wants me to talk to him. What kind of shit he's on? He wanna play Russian roulette wit' my life, Reesie thought.

"My fault, Ms. Wright. Are ya mad about me pointin' the gun at ya? And it had one bullet. Well, I guess today is yo' lucky day. Or is it? We'll see later. Ya know I wouldn't shoot ya. I love ya."

"Caelin are you on sumthin' 'cause you're actin' really bizarre?" Reesie said in a whispering manner.

"Bitch, is ya on sumthin'?" Caelin said as he slapped her again. This time, he left a handprint on her jaw.

Caelin continued to drive up Olive Boulevard to North and South Boulevard. Reesie knew this route all too well. When Caelin pulled the car into the garage of Taijeon and Sameon's house, she almost fainted.

"What's wrong, Res baby? Ya act like ya seen a ghost." Caelin asked with a sneer.

"Nothin', Caelin. Everythin's fine."

129

He grabbed her by her arm as they departed from the car.

"C'mon hoe, death is waitin' on ya behind these doors."

When Reesie entered the house, she couldn't accept as true what she saw. Mya was on her knees sucking Sameon's dick while Taijeon fucked her in the ass. She snatched away from Caelin.

"Mya get the fuck up, now! Where the fuck is yo' self-respect? What have they done to you?" Reesie inquired as she pulled her up off the floor and hugged her. She couldn't prevent the tears from running down her face. She had more than one motive for crying. She wanted to kill them all. Caelin pulled her by her hair and punched her down on the floor, but that pain didn't phase her one bit. Looking at her sister was the most hurtful thing she could envision.

"Enough of this shit," Caelin said as he pulled Reesie from the floor. "Reesie, remember them?" he said, pointing to the twins. They waved.

"You know them, Caelin?" Reesie asked, looking at him strangely.

"Of course I do. We are first cousins. Reesie Wright meet Taijeon and Sameon Ross. See, Reesie, ya never know who I know and where I know them from. Ya were in Chicago and New York being a hoe, and it caught up wit' cha. How ya feel now, hoe?"

Caelin's mental abuse became devastating. Reesie tried to block him out and only focus on Mya, but somehow Caelin voice echoed in her head.

"Taijeon, what have you done to her, you dysfunctional muthafucka? Mya, talk to me."

Mya was so exhausted, she was glad Reesie had come when she did. Her legs felt shaky and she fell straight to the floor. Reesie tried to pull her up off the floor and was unsuccessful.

"Caelin, this is a dirty game you're playin'. It's me you want. Let Mya go. I see now this was yo' way of keepin' up wit' me. That's why ya'll was lettin' them thangs go for so cheap. Believe it or not, game recognizes game. So Caelin, what now?" Reesie asked with her hands on her hips. She was fuming, and it was whatever at this point.

"Yo' Reesie, I thought I had a down ass bitch, but I see I was wrong. When you deceive Caelin Ross, it's just like deceiving God, and ya will pay dearly. Every punishment is different now, Res. That's what's up."

Reesie continued to talk to Mya, and she came around after she smacked her in the face a couple times.

"Caelin, can I take her to the bathroom and clean her up?" Reesie asked with much attitude.

"I don't give a fuck if maggots grow from the nasty bitch, them niggas is fuckin' her, not me. Long as that pussy right and tight, I'm good," Caelin said pointing to Reesie and snorting a line of coke.

Reesie continued to beg Caelin to let her clean up her friend. Finally Caelin gave in, but only under one condition.

"Taijeon, go in there wit' them."

"C'mon Caelin, it's me you want not Mya. Give us some privacy. Ten minutes is all I'm askin'."

Caelin was high as a kite by now, so Reesie knew she could pout and he'd give in.

"Res, go 'head, but if ya trip that's yo' ass and hers too," Caelin said, waving her to go.

Once inside the bathroom with the door closed and the shower running, Reesie let the toilet seat down and sat Mya on it. Just when she was about to disrobe her, Mya spoke. "Reesie, I can take off my clothes and bathe myself."

Reesie grabbed Mya and hugged her so tight. "Mya get in the shower while I call Scales on my cell phone."

She pushed number two for speed dialing Libra's cell. She knew Libra would answer her cell phone if she didn't answer the house phone.

Ring, ring!

"Hello." Libra answered on the first ring.

"Scales, listen to me. That nigga Caelin knows everything. He has Mya and me at the twins' house in U City. Call Lorenzo and tell him the de."

KNOCK! KNOCK! KNOCK! It was all Reesie and Mya heard.

Reesie dropped the phone and Caelin walked in. "I know ya was up to no good. I just gave ya enough rope to hang yo'self, bitch."

Caelin punched Reesie in the eye and she fell back into the toilet. Mya get yo' wanna be Kelly from Destiny Child's ass out the shower, like ya really take baths."

"Hello" was all Caelin heard when he picked the phone up off the floor. He said nothing but closed the phone and started beating Reesie unmercifully. While he beat her he talked to her.

"Bitch, I gotta take ya somewhere else now. Did ya tell that bitch where ya was at?" His voice became piercing.

Mya came from behind the shower curtain and hit him with the caddy. He stumbled from side to side. It really didn't faze him. Mya was still weak from the sexual activities that had taken place earlier. Taijeon came in the bathroom and pulled Mya by her hair. He wasn't forceful, because he was sweet on Mya. He didn't want to hurt her too badly.

Chapter 18

Get Down Like Ya' Live

When Libra disconnected the call from Lorenzo she wondered if she should call Mrs. Wright, but she quickly discarded the thought from her mind. *She taught us how to defend ourselves*, she thought. Once she knew the location of her sisters, she grabbed her Louis Vutton purse with the snub nose 38 special inside and jumped in the black Toyota Camry. This was the first car Mrs. Wright had purchased for her.

As she pulled away from her home, she phoned Lorenzo again.

Ring, ring!

"What's good, Lil Mama?" Lorenzo asked Libra.

"I'm not makin' no noise yet. Where you be, Lo?" Libra stated hyped up.

"On my way to get my mans. You know how we do it. We get down like we live, Lil Mama."

The thought of Keke pissed Libra the fuck off, but at this time, her sisters needed her, and she wanted any assisting that was available. She knew Caelin would kill a nigga on sight, and she had to come correct. Keke and his crew was the niggas to handle business.

"I'm goin' to wait until you call me before I do anythin'. Hey Lo, ya'll be careful."

"Good lookin' out, Lil Mama, one," Lorenzo responded, appreciating the concern.

Libra was indecisive about what to do next. Out of the clear blue sky, Slick penetrated in the head. She knew if she called him, nine times out of ten he would call Nutcase, but from the last time they had any dealings, he had made it abundantly clear he wanted nothing else to do with her. Again she quickly discarded the thought from her mind.

Caelin made Reesie and Mya go to the car, and Taijeon and Sameon tied them up as they rode to their next destination. Caelin knew Reesie had gotten a hold of Libra and their whereabouts were known, now. When he got her away from there, he was going to make her pay for everything she'd done to him. Just for the fact that she knew him, he would make her suffer. His intentions were to kill Reesie and Mya, and if the twins didn't do what they were told, they were going to die, also. He didn't give a fuck.

They took the work van and went to Ladue. Caelin figured no one would find them there. Lorenzo, Keke and Ton-Loc arrived at the house in U City, but no one was there. Libra was going to sit and watch the house across the street from Heman Park, but she was too late.

Caelin had parked the van in the garage. This house was well designed. Reesie thought, *You can be wit' somebody and still don't know a damn thing about them.* She never knew of this house, or the other house for that matter.

Caelin sat at the kitchen table, snorting another line of girl. He offered Mya and Reesie some. Mya wanted to accept but she knew Reesie would murder her before it was her time.

"Caelin don't nobody want none of that damn poison," Reesie said, furious.

"That dope fiend bitch Mya do. Look how's she lookin at this shit. C'mere and suck my dick and ya can have all the dope ya want. I heard that top piece was fire." That deal was pleasing to Mya's ears and she did exactly what he asked.

Reesie was so hurt to see her girl go out like that. She didn't give a fuck about her sucking his dick—it was

what she sucked his dick for. Mya looked at Reesie with
apologetic eyes. Reesie knew her friend was sick, and if
God permitted them to leave there alive, she would get her
some help. That was a promise she made to herself right
then and there.

In the middle of Mya sucking Caelin's dick the
twins walked into the room and wanted their dicks sucked.

"Reesie come over here and give us some jaw
action," Sameon told Reesie.

Caelin hit Sameon in the back of the head with his
gun. "Nigga, ya bet' not never disrespect me or my bitch as
long as ya breathe, ya understand, ya bitch ass puck?"
Sameon fell to the floor holding the back of his head.

"Damn, Lay Lay! I though you were through
dealing with her. You know a nigga would never, eva'
disrespect you," Sameon said looking at the blood that
oozed from his head.

It was getting late and Lorenzo saw no sign of
Caelin. He knew if he wanted info, he would have to
contact an old head that knew everything and everybody's
business.

"Dig Keke, we can't camp out here all night. That
nigga ain't comin' back here. Fam, when is the last time
you seen Jokah?" Lorenzo asked his friend.

"It's been a while derrty, but we can go by his
house and get some answers. Offer him a couple g's, he's
good. He'll tell on his mama for the right price or right
high. Think that's a lie!" declared Keke.

"We there then, nigga, 'cuz we have to find that
punk befo' he does sumthin' stupid."

With that said, the fellows kept it movin'.

The ride to Jokah's house was quiet. Lorenzo broke
the silence. "Fam, do you wanna be wit' Lil Mama?"
Lorenzo questioned Keke, trying to keep his eyes on the
road, looking back and forth at Keke then the road.

"Why you ask me that derrty?" Keke said, looking shocked.

"Nigga, answer the muthafuckin' question. Don't answer a question wit' a question, nigga." Lorenzo fussed at Keke like he was chastising a child.

"Man, I don't know what I want. I know when I see her wit' the guy Nutcase, I want her all to myself. Then she got a mouth on her that makes you wanna knock the shit of her, but she too cute to be gettin' hit on. And she's simply not having that. Lo, I don't wanna talk 'bout that now. Nigga, you need to ask yo' damn self that question. You like Reesie? Man, she is hot. Did you tap that ass or not, fam damn!" Keke asked impatiently.

"Dawg, a man never kiss and tell, didn't I tell you that be'fo?" Lorenzo said, laughing.

"Fuck that ol' fag, pop ass nigga."

"Whateva', nigga. Call it what you wanna call it. It's fo' me to know and you to find out," Lorenzo stated smiling.

They reached Jokah's house and no one answered the door. The last time Lorenzo knocked on the door, it opened slightly. He and Keke looked at each other and thought the same thing. They removed their pistols and cocked them. Keke counted to three, not making a sound. Lorenzo read his lips. On the count of three Lorenzo opened the door at a sharp swing. When they enter the apartment they weren't surprised at what they saw. Jokah was at the kitchen table shooting up.

"Damn, Jokah man, you might wanna close the door when you handlin' yo' bit'ness, mane. Muthafucka', though you expired in this bitch," Lorenzo stated as he and Keke walked all the way into the apartment.

"I'm good, young bloods. Just doin' what I do. Mindin' my own, takin' care of my own. What's good, though?" Jokah asked Lorenzo and Keke as they stood at the table.

"Tell us where Lay Lay lives. Better yet, tell us where all his houses are at. We know you know Jokah. C'mon, we gon' make it worth yo' time.

"Now young blood, ya gon' have to be ready fo' war 'cuz that lil nigga don't give a shit 'bout nothin' and nobody. Just a word from the wise. Now, how much ya got?" Jokah said, scratching his arm and licking his dry lips.

"Here's a g," Keke said pulling the money from his Ekco jacket.

Keke and Lorenzo listened with awareness as Jokah disclosed the information.

"Young blood that's the deal, don't sleep on him."

"Jokah, you bet' not be lying or yo' ass is grass," Lorenzo said as they walk out the door. The fellows were back on the road. Word had gotten around town that Pooh was fucking with Caelin. Lorenzo, not knowing how Keke really felt about Pooh, didn't want to bring the subject up but thought he would anyway.

"Dawg, since you couldn't answer the first question, answer this question. Do you know 'bout Lay Lay and Pooh?" Lorenzo stated, glancing at Keke.

"Yeah, I heard 'bout it. But you know Pooh say that's a lie. I don't give a fuck one way or the other. I just want her outta my life fo' good. The only way to do that is to kill that bitch. She's like a bad habit. That broad got too much info on me, anyway."

Lorenzo had to look at his friend and see if he was serious or what. Looking at the expression on his face, he knew he was as serious as cancer and AIDS put together. And that was serious.

"Keke, won't you see what kind of info you can get from her, which will help us a lot? Nigga, go suck her pussy or fuck the shit outta her and inquire about the situation. Tell her you can't take the rumors anymore."

Keke had to wonder if Lorenzo was serious or just plain fuckin' out of his mind.

Lorenzo and Keke went to Lorenzo's house. They chilled there a while, and Keke thought critically about what Lorenzo had said in the car. Maybe he could get some information from Pooh if he was nice to her. He called her on the phone.

Ring, ring!

"What's crackin', Pooh?" asked Keke.

"Nothin'. What's up wit' you," Pooh said, happy to hear his voice.

"I was thinkin' 'bout you. I wanna know if we could talk," asked Keke.

"We can talk about anythin' you wanna talk about, baby. Nothin' would make me more happy than workin' things out wit' you, big daddy."

"I'll see you in a minute, okay?"

"Okay, baby," stated Pooh.

Keke could not stand to be around her. He wanted out of this relationship so badly, but she knew things about him that could incriminate him and send him to prison for the rest of his life. He informed Lorenzo of his plan and told him he'd taken his advice. Keke told him he would get with him tomorrow with all the information and see if Pooh and Jokah's information coincided. Then they would take it from there.

Chapter 19

We Must Live and We Must Die

Reesie's body was in bad condition from Caelin beating her the way he did. She had wounds and bruises over her entire body. Caelin didn't give a damn. He was a heartless human being. He felt she didn't have to look good for him anymore, so what the fuck. She had betrayed him, and he had warned her, but she didn't pay him any attention.

Mya and Reesie wondered why Libra hadn't found them yet, knowing it was just a matter of time before she was coming. They couldn't stay another night with them crazy muthafucka's. Mya had performed so many sexual acts that her pussy or ass couldn't get wet anymore. Her mouth had even come to the point were it felt like cotton. Reesie was tired of fucking Caelin's unbalanced ass. She didn't know what to do. He made her do things they'd never done before. The three years they'd been together, Caelin had never asked Reesie to perform anal sex until today.

"Res, I think it's time we put some spice in our sex life," Caelin stated aggressively.

"Caelin, what you talkin about? You know I don't get down like that," Reesie said with much attitude.

"Ya don't have a choice in the matter today, Res. Ya see, I don't care how ya get down. It's goin' my way today and any other day that I let ya live, ya understand?"

Reesie looked at him with murder in her eyes, but that's all she could do because her body was worn out. Caelin still didn't give a damn. He knew he ran that ship.

"Caelin, I know we not getting down like that. I haven't done nothin' that bad to you that you would violate me that way," Reesie stated suddenly. "I know we are having problems, but damn Lay, how could you be so heartless, man?" Reesie looked at Caelin with pleading tears forming in her eyes.

"Ms. Wright, I don't give a damn about them tears. They use to make a nigga feel bad. They do nothin' to me, now. Ya might as well lay here and get what's cumin' to ya. Ya the one ask fo' it. Heartless, yes that's me. I don't care about nothin'. I saw a nigga shoot my moms in cold blood. And ya know what else? My own flesh and blood had some niggas rob me. Can you believe tha shit! And that's not all.. Bones had this ol' dope fiend ass girlfriend. Well, let say, she was suppose to be my step mom. Oh yeah, we fucked and I fell in love wit' her and she had sumthin' to do wit' the robbery. So tell me, why should I give a fuck about you? Reesie, I could talk about ya, but that wouldn't be in yo' best interest right now. Did ya forget about my man, Da Don. Them cowards must definitely pay, wit' their lives. I wouldn't have it no other way, ya dig?"

"I'm hip," was Reesie response.

Caelin always wanted to know if he had her full attention.

———————

Keke called Lorenzo bright and early that morning to verify that the information they received was correct. Pooh and Jokah had confirmed the same addresses. They would ride on that nigga today.

Ring, ring!

"Sup nigga, what's crackin?" Keke greeted Lorenzo on the other end of the phone.

"Shit nigga, you got it. If I had yo' hands, I'd cut mines off. But what's the deal?" Lorenzo joked around.

"Meet me in da hood. We can handle that today," Keke stated, not wanting to reveal too much info over the phone.

"That's what I'm talkin' 'bout, nigga. I'll see you in two and two." The line was disconnected.

The guys met in the hood. Lorenzo decided to take Keke to the house of one of the new chicks who had moved in on Semple Avenue. Keke didn't know his partner was putting it down like this, because this chick was fine as fuck. Keke had heard about her but never paid her any mind, because he was on Libra at the time that she moved into the neighborhood. But he saw his dawg had no problem being the welcome committee.

"Damn derrty you never told me about this," Keke said to Lorenzo.

"Derrty you never ask 'bout this. But we're not here to talk 'bout her. Tell me what you know," Lorenzo said, closing the book *True To the Game*, by Terri Woods.

"Man it's just like I told you on the phone. They confirmed the same spots. He has a few spots. I think we should hit the one in Ladue, then Chesterfield and then Lake St. Louis." Keke spoke anxiously.

"That bitch doin' it like that, huh! That's what's up." Lorenzo said, shaking his head. He always did that when he was in deep contemplation. "Check this out. I think we need to call Gemini. We don't know how many cats is rollin' wit' the nigga, dig! Gemini will shoot that thang and ask questions later. I'ma call him to see what's good wit' him and give him the scoop. You know he's down fo' whateva'."

"That's cool. Sounds like a plan to me," Keke said, letting Lorenzo know he was pleased with their plans.

Lorenzo, Keke and Gemini met at Lorenzo's house at eleven thirty that night. They all dressed casual. Lorenzo wore a pair of Phat Farms jeans with a sweater to match and a pair of Penny Brothers shoes and a Phat Farm jacket. Keke had on a pair of Polo jeans with a Polo shirt, Polo boots and Polo jacket, with some cold black waves. Gemini had on a pair of plain black slacks with a black muscle shirt, a brown leather coat and brown Steve Madden shoes. Cornrows braided to the back of his head. The guys didn't want to look like thugs going into a neighborhood like Ladue and take a chance on somebody calling the police.

When they arrived, they sat in the car to make sure they were at the correct address. Lorenzo parked across the street from the house, facing the house. They were in position to see everything that came and went on the block. Keke looked through Caelin's window with binoculars. He didn't see anything unusual. He saw Caelin relaxing on the couch with his hands behind his head, looking at the big screen television that was mounted on the wall.

"This nigga must think he's white, because he still got his curtains opened," Keke said, still looking through the window.

"Let me see the binoculars, man," said Gemini. "Man, the way this guy's sitting here, he ain't goin' nowhere no time soon. We gon' have to do sumthin' to make him move. Oh shit! Wait a minute, check this shit out, fam. Remember those twins we saw in New York that was staring at Reesie? Well, them the same muthafuckas' I see now."

Keke and Lorenzo reached for the binoculars. At that moment, Lorenzo reached in his pocket and threw a quarter at Caelin's truck and the alarm went off. As sure as shit stinks Sameon came outside, looked around and turned the alarm off.

"What the fuck's goin' on?" Lorenzo asked.

142

"Shit, I don't know. You tell me," Keke replied. After Sameon went back into the house, Lorenzo threw more quarters at the truck. The fellows decided that this would be the time to make their move.

This time, Taijeon came outside and disarmed the alarm. Gemini came from behind the truck with the nickel-plated nine-millimeter with the silence pointed at Taijeon's head.

"Don't even think 'bout it, pat'na," Gemini whispers to Taijeon. "Don't bullshit me. Who the fuck in the house and don't try me, nigga. You will die wit' yo' nuts in yo' mouth. Now you can play wit' me if you wanna," Gemini stated to Tai without blinking an eye.

"Yo', I don't know what you're talkin' about, playa," Taijeon replied with a trembling voice.

"This is my last time asking you, ol' bitch ass nigga. The next time I ask you, you gon' feel sumthin' hot inside yo' ass," Gemini said while pressing the nine into his head harder.

"Man, it' two lil chicks down in the basement."

"Who the fuck else? How many mo' niggas?" Gemini stated, pressing even harder and leaving a print.

"Man, my brother and cousin. It's three of us all together, dawg," Taijeon said irritated.

When Keke and Lorenzo saw Gemini lead Taijeon in the house, they were right behind them.

Just as they were about to open the side door, Sameon came out the door. Lorenzo grabbed him but he let off a shot. That's when Caelin came running to the door with his Smith and Wesson. It sounded like the Fourth of July in Ladue. Hearing those shots, Reesie knew somebody had come to rescue them. Caelin shot Keke in his right shoulder, and he moaned in pain. Caelin locked the door and ran to where the girls were, and the guys couldn't get in. Caelin went into the room and started talking to Reesie and Mya.

"Reesie, I told ya if I can't have ya, no one could. I will kill ya first befo' I let another man have ya. Mya, I don't care about ya one way or another."

After he finished that last sentence, he shot Mya in the stomach. Reesie cried out for her friend. The guys heard the gunshots and it frighten them to think what and who that could be. They didn't have a long list to pick from. They knew it could be Mya or Reesie. Lorenzo shot the lock off the basement door and it flung off.

Keke still tried to wrestle with Taijeon even with a bleeding shoulder. He shot Taijeon in the head and one shot killed him instantly. Gemini, holding Sameon by the collar, made him lead him to the girls. Lorenzo chased Caelin, firing bullets at him. Once Caelin was out of sight, Lorenzo went back to join the others. He was not pleased by what he saw.

Reesie was badly beaten and had been shot three times. Mya was cover with blood, also. Lorenzo and Gemini took the ladies pulse, and they were still breathing. Keke still had Sameon. They heard footsteps coming down the stairs, and Keke silenced everybody. They knew it wasn't Caelin, because whoever it was had on heels. The footsteps came closer, and all they heard was Reesie mumbling, "It's Scales. Please don't shoot."

"Lil Mama, is that you?" Lorenzo yelled at the top of the stairs.

"Yes, it's me." When Libra made it down to the basement, she had her .25 in her hand. She cried like a baby at what she saw.

"I have to get them to the hospital. Somebody help me, please. She checked Reesie's pulse first, then Mya's.

"C'mon Keke, help me get them to the car. Please hurry!"

144

Keke saw Libra trying to pick up Reesie and told Sameon, "Nigga, you bet' not move or that will be yo' last move."

Libra watched Keke release Sameon and said, "You don't have to worry about that fag pop ass nigga movin' again." She gave him two shots to the head, leaving half his brains hanging out.

The guys put both girls in Libra's Camry. She rushed them to St. Mary's hospital. On the way to the hospital Libra prayed to God like never before.

"Father God above, please look down here on your small people, like Reesie, Mya and myself. Lord, please don't take them from me. Everythin' you given me that I love, you take it away before I'm ready to let it go. Heavenly Father, you took my mama away, but you sent me a blessing by replacing her with a mother figure in Mrs. Wright. Lord, I need them in my life. Please give them a chance to know what they really want. Lord Jesus, I will leave this life that I'm living in a heartbeat if I can have the two people that mean so much to me back. Lord, you say we have not because we ask not. Father, I'm askin' in Jesus' name. Amen."

Libra heard Reesie say "Amen," and right then and there, she knew God had answered her prayer. Libra knew she had to call Mrs. Wright at this point. She knew she wasn't going to be pleased with the news that she was about to deliver. She looked at both her sisters and told them to hold on. She pulled the Nextel phone from her Gap purse. She pushed the number three on speed dial.

Ring, ring!

"Hey Ma," Libra said to Mrs. Wright trying to sound calm.

"Libra, what is it? Why are you're calling me at this time of morning? Baby, are you girls okay?" Mrs. Wright was worried to death. She didn't play when it came to her girls. She asked question after question.

"Mama! I'm on my way to St. Mary's hospital. Please meet me there," Libra said to Mrs. Wright, crying.

"Baby, I'm on my way as we speak. Take your time and drive carefully. I'll see you soon. Libra sweetie, I love you," Mrs. Wright said with motherly love. "I love you more, Ma," Libra shared. She disconnected the call and answered her other line.

Ring, ring!

"Hello."

"Ladybug, you made it to the hospital yet?" Keke asked with great concern.

"We're almost there. Are you comin' to the hospital to get checked out yo'self?" Libra asked before realizing what she said.

"Fo' sho', Ladybug. We're on our way now. We had to clean ourselves up. You know what I mean. I'm gonna go to the hood doctor. He'll take care of this. It's nothin'. I'll live."

"That's good because I don't think I can do this alone. I'm here," Libra said, pulling in to the emergency entrance. "See you when you get here."

She disconnected the call. Libra left the car running and went to get help.

The nurses came to get both girls immediately and took them to the trauma area. Libra saw Mrs. Wright when she pulled up at the same entrance she'd entered. Mrs. Wright jumped out of her car and left it running, as well. She saw Libra running to her and heard her crying, "Tell me its gon' be alright, Ma. Please tell me its gon' be alright!"

"Pie, it's going to be all right, baby. Stop all that crying and carrying on so you can tell me what happened to my babies," Mrs. Wright said to Libra, trying to sound strong.

But deep down inside she wanted to cry at the same time. She and Libra walked to the waiting room. Mrs. Wright instructed Libra to have a seat.

"Now Libra, tell me what happen' without all that crying, baby." She wiped the tears from her face.

Libra explained everything to Mrs. Wright without leaving out a detail. They knew she didn't play that lying shit.

"There's nothing you girls can't tell me. Regardless of what the situation is. I'm the only one got you all's back, even if it's bad. I'ma stand up for you and then whip that ass later if you're wrong."

When Libra finished, Mrs. Wright went to the nurse's station, searching for news of her daughters' condition.

"Mrs. Wright, the doctor will be out soon to give you information. They're still operating on the patients."

That's what she'd heard an hour ago. The guys were in the waiting room with Libra when Mrs. Wright returned. Libra introduced Mrs. Wright to the fellows.

"There's no introduction needed. I feel like I know you fellas already. I've heard so much about ya'll."

Mrs. Wright didn't say anything else when she saw the doctor walking their way.

"Hi. Is this the family of Reesie Wright and Mya Williams?" Dr. Jackson asked.

"Yes it is, doctor. I'm the mother of both girls. How are they and please, don't sugar coat it. Let me have it like it really is," Mrs. Wright demanded looking serious and firmly shaking the doctor's hand.

"I will do nothing but that, madam. I'm also here to report Reesie Wright's condition. And by the way, I'm Dr. Jackson," he said, shaking her hand again. "She's in critical condition. The bullet to the head did a lot of damage. You have a very important decision to make," Dr. Jackson said, looking at Mrs. Wright and everyone else that was present in the room. He sounded distressed.

"I have done everything I can for Reesie. There nothing else that can be done. We do have a better chance at saving the twin's life than hers. You have twenty-four hours to decide if you want to save Reesie's life or the babies. The babies are fully developed now. She was in her seventh month. They are still small at this point but they have a better chance than Reesie," Dr. Jackson said assuring her he was doing everything he could.

"Doctor, what about my other baby, Mya Williams."

"Mya's still in surgery. The only thing I know at this point is that the process is going good. Her doctor will be down later to give you more information. Just keep God in your life first," Dr. Jackson said as he walked away.

Mrs. Wright and Libra stayed at the hospital until six o'clock that evening. The fellows left and brought them back something to eat. They stay a while longer and then left to ear-hustle on the street about Caelin's whereabouts. They hit every neighborhood lounge, telling the owners to keep their ears and eyes open. Mrs. Wright didn't have too much time to make her decision about her daughter's life. She couldn't see herself losing her only daughter, but then she still had two daughters and the twins. But Reesie was her baby that she had carried for nine months. Reesie was her baby that she had felt moving inside of her. She stayed in labor ten hours with Reesie, her baby. The way Mrs. Wright felt at that moment, she wouldn't wish this kind of pain on her worst enemy.

Mama, we gon' pray and ask God to guide us and help us make the right decisions," Libra said, hugging Mrs. Wright.

148

Chapter 20

The Choices We Make in Life

Mrs. Wright hoped that Reesie would show some kind of improvement before it was time for her to make the most important decision she'd ever have to make in her life. Reesie's recovery had come to a halt. However, Mya was making great process. Libra and Mrs. Wright were grateful for that. Mrs. Wright and Libra talked about the decision they had to make. They agreed to let the babies live.

"Libra baby, I guess you were right when you said Reesie got to live some of her life. We should let the twins have life and enjoy life as their mother did."

But before they made it final, they went and talked to Mya. She was doing fine, expect for the excruciating pain she was in. They all went to see Reesie an hour before her life was about to end.

Mrs. Wright walked in the room followed by her friend, Mr. John, and Libra pushing Mya in a wheelchair. They gathered around Reesie's bed and talked to her. Even though she was in a coma, she knew what was going on around her. Reesie was dreaming that the nurse brought her babies into the room with her and they had the prettiest creamy chocolate skin you ever wanted to see. It was a girl and boy. They were so precious. The nurse gave Reesie her baby girl and gave Caelin their baby boy, and he ran away with her son and she never got to see him again.

In her dream, she heard herself telling Caelin, "Please don't take my babies from me. They are all I have."

Caelin did not pay any attention to Reesie and he told her, "You will never know how my son looks. Look at

149

ya. You are a poor excuse for a woman." Caelin laughed in Reesie's face.

She reached for her baby, but Caelin got away. She called the nurse and the nurse turned out to be Pooh. Pooh look at her and she laughed, too. Reesie remembered the cut Libra had left on her face.

The others in the room noticed her stressing out and wondered if she was responding to them. Reesie fought long and hard to retrieve her baby from Caelin, but she didn't get him, and she finally gave up the fight. The monitors started beeping fast, and the nurses and doctors ran into her room, telling everybody they had to leave. There was nothing they could do. Reesie was gone.

Dr. Jackson didn't want to be the bearer of bad news, but that was his job. He had seen too many cases like this one. It hurt him badly, because he lost his daughter to an abusive boyfriend, and there was nothing he could do as a doctor or father once God had removed her from the face of this earth.

The news wasn't taken very well. Mrs. Wright had to be admitted in the hospital for high blood pressure. Mya blamed herself, because she felt that Reesie had come looking for her. Libra's heart was saddened, knowing that she would never see her sister-friend again. But she knew that revenge is best served cold, and Libra had every intention on serving Caelin "hard and good and below zero. 'Cause this is what it is."

Before Libra could go to the waiting room to tell Lorenzo, Gemini and Keke what had happened, they were already walking into Reesie's room. Lorenzo removed his red STL baseball cap from his head; put it over his face and let the tears flow freely down his face. Gemini walked over to Mya, who was sitting in the wheelchair and started rubbing her back. Keke walked over and hugged Libra. She didn't refuse his embrace. Mr. John let the tears flow as freely as anyone.

Libra broke Keke's embrace and found Dr. Jackson to inquire about the twins and Mrs. Wright's condition. They wanted to keep Mrs. Wright overnight for observation. The babies were doing fine though they were born premature. One of the babies was smaller than the other one. They both were going to have to remain in the hospital for a few months. Libra, Mya and Mrs. Wright knew they were blessed when God gave them two lives and took one. They all agreed to raise the twins. It was a girl and boy, and Libra named them Miracle and Chance. They sat in Mrs. Wright's room, waiting for the doctor to let them see the babies. Libra came up with the names, and everyone agreed.

"Libra baby, why did you come up with those names?" asked Mrs. Wright.

"The way I see it is, the Lord performed a miracle and blessed them both at a chance at life," Libra said

Even though Miracle and Chance were just born, they resembled Reesie a great deal. Mya knew she had to get herself together for the twins' sake. She didn't want her niece and nephew seeing her high. She would go straight to rehab when she got out of the hospital. Mrs. Wright would give the twins the best life she could, but right now she had to make plans to put her baby six feet under, and she promised that somebody would pay one way or another. Mr. John felt like he was the daddy. Even though he wasn't Reesie's real father, he had always treated her, Libra and Mya like he was their father. Mr. John was a truck-driver, and he drove all over the country. Mr. John and Mrs. Wright were married through common law. They had been together a while.

Lorenzo was amazed at how much the twins looked like Reesie.

"Lo, I want to know … No, let me rephrase that. We would like to know if you would be the twins' godfather, because we know how much you cared for Reesie," Libra asked him with tears in her eyes.

"I wouldn't have it no other way, Lil Mama," Lorenzo said, never removing his eyes from the babies.

"What part of the babies' lives will I be a part of?" asked Keke.

"We'll be the uncles," answered Gemini with a giant smile on his face.

"Ladybug, can I holla at you in the hall, please?" questioned Keke.

Libra asked the others to excuse her and she left the room with Keke.

"You know, the fellas and I got this shit on lock. That nigga will not walk these streets. We done holla'd at everybody and got people on the lookout. I want you to lay low fo' a minute till we get this bitch ass nigga."

"Keke, I'm good. Mya and I are movin' back home wit' Ma to help wit' the babies and get Mya back on track, and also, I have to make sure Mama take her medication. We're thinkin' about selling the house and gettin' sumthin' bigger," Libra informed Keke.

Lorenzo and Gemini exited the nursery and informed Keke it was time to roll out. They said their goodbyes and kept it movin'.

Chapter 21

Tha Home Going

Libra did everything she could do to make this process as easy as possible for Mrs. Wright. No matter what she would do, she couldn't take the place of Reesie and she would never try. She wanted Mrs. Wright to know she was there for her when she needed her, the same way she had been a mother to her and Mya all these years. Mya wanted to stay away until she got herself together. Libra and Mrs. Wright informed Mya that this was nothing to go through by herself, and they were there for her no matter what. She still seemed to distance herself.

Gemini, Lorenzo and Keke were very supportive of the girls after their loss. Lorenzo went to see the twins every day, taking them big teddy bears and all kinds of colorful things. Gemini wanted to help Mya get back on the right track. Keke knew Libra would never trust him again, so he tried being a friend instead of a lover.

Reesie's funeral was in a couple of days, and still there was no word on Caelin. No one had seen or heard from him. That was best for him. He knew he was on the most wanted list around the Lou. He would be caught by one of these vigilantes..

Libra and Lorenzo went to Children's Hospital everyday. The twins' progress was blessed. They were eating well and gaining weight. That was a blessing to Libra in itself. Mrs. Wright was doing as well as could be expected. She didn't go see the twins every day. She wanted to sit in her room. She had a lovely room, with lots of photos of the girls. She even had a photo of them at a third grade school dance. She also had several photos of herself, Linda and Mia. Her grandbabies reminded her of her baby a lot, and that was too much. Mya went to the hospital to visit them when no one else was there; and that was just about never. Between Libra, Lorenzo and Keke, someone was there with them at all times. The twins would be alone for the first time on the day of Reesie's funeral.

Libra took care of all the funeral arrangements with the help of Lorenzo. He was a blessing to her friend. She only wished Reesie had met him first, instead of Caelin. But everything happens for a reason. That's what they said.

Mya and Libra moved some of their things home. Libra was in her room, arranging things to her liking and listening to music. That's how they got down in the Wright household—cleaning up, especially on a Saturday morning, and cleaning up when the three of them stayed home. She sat down at her computer and checked her email. She hadn't done that in days. She had three inbox messages and they all read:

Blessings. I don't know what to say at a time like this, but I want you to know that my prayers are with you, as well as Reesie's family. Keep your head up and be the strong black sister you are.

Libra's eyes watered at the thought of Nutcase. She really didn't know how much she was in love with him until the breakup. If there was a chance with Nutcase, she would go for it, but he was about business and he needed to feel that sense of trust. She felt it would be too much right now to try and gain his trust after all this time. It had been four months now, and there had been no kind of communication between them—none whatsoever.

She also had a lot on her plate right now, with Reesie's death, the twins, Mya and Mrs. Wright, along with running back and forth to the hospital every day. Libra would have to explain being in Keke's presence every day, regardless of what the situation was. That would be too much energy wasted, and time is not on anyone's side.

She opened the next email, which was also from Nutcase, and it read:

> *Blessings. I hope you are reading your emails or two-way pager, but I suppose not because none of my messages have been answered. Your cell number is still the same, but all I get is your voice mail. I have left several messages. Contact me please. Here's my numbers. Call me any time.*

He left his home, cell and business numbers.

Libra was too outdone. Her panties weren't touching her anywhere. She began to pray to herself.

> *"Lord, I'm askin' you for strength and guidance. Father God, I'm askin' anything that is not of you, keep it away from me, in yo' name. In Jesus' name. Amen. Amen."*

Libra's mind drifted back to when Keke told her, "Everyone has his or her own relationship with God," and at that very moment she realized that this was so very true.

She opened the last message, which was again from Nutcase, and it read:

> *Blessings. I heard about Reesie, and if there is anything I can do, please feel free to contact me anytime. And I mean that literally.*

"He ain't gotta tell me twice," Libra thought out loud.

Again, she didn't want to seem anxious. She put her pride aside and called Nutcase.

Ring, ring! Ring, ring!

Libra waited for the voice message: "Hi, this is Tyron. Please leave a name and number and the nature of your call, and I promise to return your call at my earliest convenience. Blessings!"

Beep!

"Hi Tyron. This is Libra. Call me when it's convenient for you. You have a blessed day."

Libra hung up the phone and put some volume on her radio. She was listening to a mixed CD that Reesie, Mya and she used to listen to while riding around, chilling. Tomorrow would be the last day she would get to see her sister-friend. Libra knew Mya would break down at Reesie's funeral. All she wanted to do was be there for her, as well as for Mrs. Wright.

The Day of the Funeral

Reesie's birthday was the next day, February 14th, Valentines Day. No one had said a word about it. It was sunny outside, but a bit chilly. Overall, a nice day for St. Louis in the wintertime.

Mrs. Wright, Libra, Mya and Mr. John rode in a white stretch Escalade limo with every feature you could imagine. The fellows—Lorenzo, Keke, Gemini, Ton-Loc and Tiffany—rode in their own limo. Greater Mount Zion Baptist Church was over flowing with people. Every last seat in the house was occupied. People were even standing along the walls. The ushers put chairs at the end of each aisle.

Libra with Lorenzo's help did an awesome job arranging the funeral. He was pleased, as well. She organized the order of the service skillfully. Reesie's coffin was very beautiful. The baby pink coffin brightened the entire church, along with all the flowers and the big Winnie the Pooh balloons. Libra said Reesie was an angel, and all angels wear white and go to heaven. What lay inside was beauty, and nothing could take that away from her, dead or alive—not even all that ass kicking Caelin had inflicted on her.

Reesie was dressed in an all white Dolce and Gabbana pantsuit with baby pink stripes. Her hands were lying across her breast with cotton candy nail polish. A veil lay over the coffin. On her left side was a photo of Libra, Mya and Mrs. Wright. On her right side was a photo of Libra, Mya and her in third grade at a school dance. In between was a photo of her twins. Flowers were everywhere.

Mrs. Wright, Libra and Mya sat on the first row dressed like Reesie. Mr. John also sat with them. The fellows followed suit and sat right behind them. Lorenzo didn't say anything to Libra about security. He had that part on lock down. Well, he thought he did.

Little did Lorenzo know that Libra had gotten in touch with Nutcase's security team from her birthday party. They did not play games. If you tripped, you were sure to leave with a pumpkin head. There wasn't anything nice about that. Caelin would have to go through a lot to get into this home-going service. Nutcase arranged for his security team to work the funeral. He took very good care of his team and their families. Loyalty had kept that establishment together all these years. New friends were never Nutcase's thing. He kept a low profile. He was in a class all by himself. He was every woman's dream and many men's nightmare.

Libra sang, *It So Hard to Say Goodbye to Yesterday*. The girls used to sit in bed with Mrs. Wright and watch all the old movies and sitcoms. *Cooley High* was one of Reesie's favorites and *Good Times, Sanford and Son* and *The Jeffersons* were part of her daily after school routine. She said it reminded her of Libra, Mya and herself. They were friends forever, and only death could separate them. Libra sung that song with all of her heart and soul. She got down. She could be the next America Idol and make Simon eat his heart out.

Libra told herself earlier in the week that Mya was going to break down, and she did just that. Libra was her backbone, as well as every other bone in her body. She was the support system that Mya needed. Mrs. Wright held up well. The burial was the last chance to see their love one before the body was placed in the ground.

Mya wanted to do something special. She went and purchased two white doves and kept them in a cage. Releasing the doves would be the last thing Mya did to complete Reesie's home going. As Mya released the two doves, Lorenzo did the same with his two.

Back at the hospital, the twins were dressed in white and pink, also. They had baby Dolce and Gabbana. Libra even had a hat made for Chance and a T-shirt made with pictures of their mother on the front and back. Nurse Sasha commented on how lovely the twins looked.

Sasha was filling in for nurse Nicki, who had called in sick. They were good friends. Sasha worked on 7-East, a different floor from Nicki's floor. They kept each other up-to-date on all the gossip. She was taking the babies' temperatures when her cell phone vibrated on her hip. Sasha knew she wasn't supposed to have her cell phone on while she was at work, because it was against hospital policy.

"What's up Sasha?" said the voice on the other end.

"Everything's clear. The funeral's going to last a while. That will give ya'll some time with them," Sasha whispered. "Lanitra, do everything I told you to do and it will work out perfectly." That was Sasha's last statement. She disconnected the call.

Libra called to check on the twins.

"7–West. Sasha speaking, how can I help you?" Sasha spoke professionally and pleasantly.

"I'm sorry I didn't catch your name correctly. Sasha is it?" Libra asked.

"Yes that is correct. Who am I speaking with, please?" Sasha said getting annoyed with the question.

"I'm Libra Love. I'm calling to check on the Wright twins. They are my niece and nephew. Are you a new nurse, because your name doesn't sound familiar?" Libra asked with concern in her voice.

"Yes, I was on call. Their regular nurse called in sick. I'm covering her shift," Sasha said, still trying to sound pleasant, but the questions were killing her. "Their condition is the same. They just had their feeding. They will more than likely sleep all day. Ms. Love if anything changes, I'll make sure to give you a call. I was left strict orders to phone you if there are any changes in their condition, day or night."

"It's nice to know services are being rendered as ordered."

With that Libra disconnected the call, but didn't feel right about it.

Sasha looked at the other nurse and doctor in the room and told them it was time they left. She had a feeling Libra was coming to the hospital. They agreed, paid Sasha for the information and her services and left the hospital.

Libra followed her first mind, the way Mrs. Wright had taught her, and went to the hospital immediately after the burial. She checked on the twins and went to the nurses' station. She asked to speak with the head nurse.

"Yes, what can I do for you Ms. Love?" asked the nurse putting the pen down.

"In the future I would like to be informed when the Wright twins are going to have a different nurse. Please don't let this happen again."

Libra left the nurse standing with her mouth open and kept it movin'.

159

When she made it back to the twins' room, she told Sasha she could leave and that she would call her if she needed her. Sasha did just that, with no reply. Libra stayed the night with the twins. Periodically, she called to check on Mya and Mrs. Wright.

Chapter 22

What's Meant to Be Will Be

Libra sat and read the twins a story. That's basically what she did all the while she was there. She made sure she had taken their pictures in the outfits she had bought for them. She showed the twins the funeral services on her digital camera and hooked it up to the television so the twins could watch. Believe it or not, they paid attention to Libra talking to them and showing them the entire poster board of their mother. She was interrupted when the nurse buzzed in and asked if it would be okay to send Tyron Cross back. That was pleasing to her ears.

"Yes, of course," she said through the intercom, but on the inside, she was screaming, "Hell muthafuckin' yeah!"

She checked herself in the mirror to make sure she was in place, because earlier, Nutcase was looking quite nice. Libra also knew he would look stunning when he walked in, and she was totally accurate.

He'd changed from earlier. The black Kenneth Cole suit he had worn to the funeral was tailor-made. He entered the twins' room rocking a pair of faded Girbaud jeans with a black and white Girbaud button-up shirt, covered with a black Girbaud blazer. The collar of his shirt lay over the collar of his blazer, and he sported a pair of black and white Jordan's. He was well put together.

Libra introduced Nutcase to the twins. At once, he took to them. They brought back memories of his children. He still wanted kids, but with the precisely right person and loyalty was first in his book. It was time for the twins' feeding, and Nutcase assisted Libra. They changed their diapers and the twins drifted back to sleep.

"Libra, would you like to go grab something to eat while the twins are sleep?" asked Nutcase.

"Yes, we can go to the cafeteria. That way, I won't have to leave them. We can bring our food back to the room, if that's okay wit' you," Libra replied.

"I was thinking we could go somewhere and talk, maybe have a drink," Nutcase responded.

"Tyron I really don't wanna leave them. They have been here all day by themselves without any family. I called to check on them earlier, and the nurse that was here didn't sit well wit' me. You understand?" Libra asked Nutcase with a serious concern in her voice.

"That's fine. I understand perfectly."

Nutcase and Libra stayed up the whole night talking. He stayed all night with her and the twins. Libra enjoyed herself with Nutcase. Even though she was stressed, he eased her mind. He made her feel like everything was going to be okay. She forgot what it was to laugh. She hadn't done it in a while.

"Libra, explain to me what happened to Reesie. You know I will do everything I can to make things comfortable for you and the babies. If we're going to be a part of each other's lives, we need to know what's going on with each other. I'm not trying to run your life. I want to be a part of your life. I love you, and it's nothing I can do about it. I tried erasing you from my mind, but I can't. I'm willing to put the past behind us and start a future with you. Yesterday is history, tomorrow is a mystery and today is a gift. That's why it is called the present unknown. I know you need time to think about everything. I'm not in a rush as long as you keep it honest with me," Nutcase stated from the bottom of his heart.

"Tyron I want nothing more than to be wit' you. But right now may not be the right time. I don't want what happened to us the first time to come between us again. Wait a minute. Let me rephrase that. There is nothin' goin' on wit' Keke and me, but he do spend a lot of time wit' the twins. I tend to see him quite often since Reesie's death, and I don't want you to have any doubt in yo' mind about my faithfulness. This is so ironic, but after the breakup, I realized how much I was in love wit' you, but when you emailed me and the subject was 'It's over,' I let you have it yo' way."

Libra removed herself from her seat and went over to Chance's bed to check on him. Nutcase had the strangest look on his face when Libra turned to face him.

"Pretty I didn't email you and say no shit like that, but I was wondering why you emailed me, 'Already let go.' It wasn't until a week later when I found out Desha was the one sending you those emails. You know, she had to be dismissed. I don't play that dishonest crap. She's out of my life, and I'm looking for a future with you and the twins and only you can make that happen. So what do you say?" Tyron asked Libra, extending his hand to her to come where he was.

"I'm willin' to take one day at a time," Libra said, sitting on Tyron's lap, with her arms wrapped around his neck, kissing him passionately.

Keke walked in the room while Libra and Tyron were doing the tongue war. He didn't interrupt; he exited the room and waited for them to finish before he reentered. Lorenzo stopped at the front desk to check on the babies' progress. The nurse informed him that Libra had stayed the night and he proceeded to the room. Libra and Nutcase decided to go change clothes and give the guys some time with the twins. Keke was unhappy with what he saw, but there was nothing he could do about it. Libra's mind was made up. It was Nutcase she wanted.

Lorenzo told Libra he and Keke would stay a while, and Gemini was on his way to bring Mya. That was good to hear. Libra asked Nutcase to excuse her while she spoke with the fellows, and he did just that, exiting to the hall and going to the nurse's station.

"I thank ya'll so much for being here," Libra said, looking at Keke and Lorenzo. "Call me when ya'll leave 'cause I don't want them left alone."

"It will be a while, 'cause Mom's on her way, also," Lorenzo stated. Keke never said a word.

"That's cool. And thanks again, guys, for being here." With that said, Libra kept it movin'.

Chapter 23

Keep Yo' Enemies Close

Pooh did everything she could do to get back with Keke. Keke didn't have a desire for her in any shape, form or fashion. Yes, she was pretty, but she wasn't Libra. The streets were finally talking, and Keke didn't like what he was hearing about Pooh. News from the streets was more reliable then the actual news. He thought he would play it by ear and see what happened. If he found out the streets were correct, which he was almost certain they were, there would be one less person on the streets. They say "keep your enemies close," and that was what he planned on doing.

Thinking about moving back in with her for the time being was something he didn't want to do. Keke knew the only way he was going to find out if Pooh had any involvement with Caelin was to keep her nearby. He had to get this guy! Caelin made people lives hectic, and he had tormented so many people. He was hazardous to the health of the community.

Word on the streets was Pooh knew where Caelin was. She was his right hand woman, and for some bizarre reason, Keke could believe that. He was a little bewildered about the situation. He couldn't understand why she always made herself available to him when Caelin was a part of her life. But then, that could be a trap. Caelin was a grimy ass nigga, but game recognizes game.

Keke made his way to the hospital to see the twins. Two months had passed, and they were getting bigger and looking more like their mother. They had Caelin's dark complexion. When he entered the room, everyone was there, even that nigga he didn't want to see. The room was bright, and you could tell it was springtime outside. Nurse Nicki informed them that the twins would be released soon. The doctor was planning on letting them go home by the end of the week. That was music to Libra's ears.

"Lo, let me holla at you and Gemini," Keke said, walking to the hallway. "Man we gotta get that nigga Caelin be'fo them babies go home.. I think that bitch Pooh knows where he's at. I decided to move back in wit' her so that I can keep an eye on her."

"Man if that's the case, you think you should stay under the same roof as the bitch, fam?" Gemini asked with great concern. "Keep yo' pistol close."

"I ain't worry 'bout that hoe. I want that nigga." Keke confirmed.

"Keep me up on everythin' derrty, 'cuz I'm blasting at anythin' that moves the wrong way, ya hear me?" Lorenzo said, giving them dap. In the middle of the conversation, Keke saw Sasha walking to the nurse's station.

"Dig fam, I'm about to find out everythin' we need to know. Sasha has been throwing that pussy at me fo' years, and she sings like a bird. The whole time Pooh and I was together, she made it known that she will do anythin' to be on a nigga's team. She always stayed the night at our house when Pooh and I first got together. She always wore that tiny shit so I could see that fat ass of hers. It's on and poppin', fam."

Keke left the fellows standing and walked to where Sasha was.

"What's up, Sasha," Keke greeted her." How long you been workin' here, Ma."

"Hey, what's up Lamar? I've been working here for six months, now," Sasha said as she blushed.

166

"You still look good, Ma." Keke said, complimenting her.

"Lamar, what are you doing here?" Sasha asked, knowing why he was there. She didn't want him to know she knew about the twins and whose babies they were. Sasha hadn't forgotten that ass beaten Reesie rendered to her at the liquor store.

"What you doin' later? You wanna go have a drink or sumthin'?" Keke inquired.

"My shift doesn't end until seven tonight," Sasha responded.

"That's cool. Here's my number. Call me. I'll pick you up," Keke said, writing his cell number down and giving her the sheet of paper.

"Okay Lamar, I'll do that," Sasha said accepting the paper. She walked away and Keke's eyes followed her ass until she was out of sight.

When he went back in the room, Libra and Nutcase were about to leave. Deep on the inside, Keke was hurt, and he was hoping there was still a chance for them.

"Keke baby, what have you been doing with yourself lately. I haven't heard from you," Mrs. Wright said, walking over to him and giving him a motherly hug.

"I've been try'na keep a low profile. That's all, Mrs. Wright," Keke said returning the hug.

"I want all you kids to go out and enjoy yourselves for a change. I'm going to stay with my grandbabies tonight. Go on! Do something! Have a good time," Mrs. Wright said to them all.

Libra was already gone. Gemini waited on Mya to finish changing Miracle's diaper, and they left. Keke followed suit. Lorenzo stayed a while longer and kept Mrs. Wright company.

Gemini and Mya went on the Ameristar Casino boat in St. Charles to eat. Keke went to North Oaks Bowling

Alley on Lucas and Hunt Boulevard and Natural Bridge to shoot some pool, throw darts, and also to get his drink on until it was time to pick Sasha up from work. Libra and Nutcase went back to his place to relax.

Tyron had redecorated the house entirely. Libra entered the bedroom and loved what she saw. He had a cherry wood post bed with a matching chest, dresser and night stands. She tried to jump into the bed, but it was too high. There was a stepping stool on the side to help her climb into the king-size bed with Nutcase right by her side. She felt like a queen lying in the bed. Nutcase noticed how restful Libra seemed, and he joined her. When he lay next to her, she cuddled under him at once, and he welcomed her with open arms.

Libra just wanted to lie there and never leave his arm, but she knew in reality that all things come to an end. That's what they say. Libra turned to face Nutcase. When she looked in his eyes, a genuine guy appeared before her. Just looking at him at that moment, she knew he was hers. She could ask him to move a mountain, and he would do so or die trying.

"Tell me what you're thinking about, Pretty," Nutcase asked her, moving the hair from her eyes. He noticed that she was letting her hair grow. He almost thought it was a weave, because her hair is always the bomb, even on her bad hair days.

"I have so many things goin' through my head, baby. Sometimes I don't know if I'm comin' or goin'," Libra said with her big, sad, puppy dog eyes. "Darkness, I do have something to ask you," Libra stated, now sitting up in the bed and breaking Nutcase's hug.

"Damn baby, it must be important, because you broke lose from me," Nutcase stated playfully. Nutcase didn't see Libra's beautiful smile that brightened the entire universe and her dimples that was like the sun.

"Tyron, on the real baby, this hoe ass nigga can't get away wit' what he did to my sistahs. He didn't even give a fuck about his babies. He's cold-blooded man," Libra said with hate in her tone.

Nutcase knew she was serious as can be. In addition to that, he adored the ghetto luv in Libra.

"Nutcase, be on the look-out for Caelin and have yo' people do the same. He done got little. He's nowhere to be found. I don't want ya'll to kill him. Let me have that pleasure, and I can't wait. That killer is gonna suffer like he made my sistahs suffer. Baby, say you will help me?" Libra asked with pleading eyes.

Nutcase was already on that. He was known everywhere. He always said money talks and bullshit walks. His money talked, please believe that. Tyron Nutcase Cross was a big boy. He played with big toys and he carried large things, if you know what I mean. Caelin Ross was going to be found. He had caused the woman he loved too much pain, and he had a problem with that.

"Pretty, pump your brakes and breathe easy," Nutcase barked at Libra, trying to calm her down, while massaging her feet. "Don't worry about that. Your only concern is those babies, Mya and Mrs. Wright. That's a handful right there."

Libra knew she needed not to say anything more about the situation, and she didn't.

"I'll keep you updated. Don't go trying to be Inspector Gadget and carrying on," Nutcase said teasing.

Libra couldn't lie there another second without touching this man's body. She removed her feet off Nutcase's lap and crawled on her hands and knees to him at the bottom of the bed. When she was face-to-face with Nutcase, she kissed him seductively on the tip of his nose. Nutcase grabbed Libra and positioned her with him on top of her. As their tongues went around like a merry-go-round in each other's mouths, Libra started sucking his tongue. She felt his hardness against her, and it felt wonderful. Libra rubbed Nutcase's baldhead and pushed his head down to her wetness. Nutcase had Libra reaching for things that weren't in sight. Libra reached over her head and turned on the radio. The sweet sounds of Jill Scott filled the room. She was singing about how her man woos her, pleases her and teases her. Libra made love to Nutcase like dick was going out of style. Or could it be that it had been a long time for her?

Keke picked Sasha up from work as scheduled. He took her to Dave and Busters.

"So Keke, what's up with you and Pooh?" Sasha asked, eating her last french fry. Keke thought he would play on her intelligence, because she was naïve at times.

"I tried to make our relationship work, but Pooh's on some other bullshit and I ain't got time, you know what I mean Shawty?" Keke said, sipping his grey goose and cranberry juice. "Do you think I would be here wit' you if we were together? I don't get down like that, Ma. I need a down ass chick on my team," Keke said, watching Sasha drink her Corona beer.

"I know what you mean, Keke. I guess that's why I'm by myself. Because men play too many games."

Sasha wanted to enlighten Keke concerning Pooh and Caelin, but she could lose her job, and furthermore she could lose her life. If Caelin knew she'd played him out, she would never breathe again, but being with Keke she felt a sense of security. She would wait and play this out.

Nurse Nicki asked Mrs. Wright to sign the release papers for her grandbabies So that she could take them home. That was one of the happiest days of her life. Lorenzo, Keke and Gemini were there to make sure Mrs. Wright, Libra, Mya and the twins reached home safely. When they arrived at Mrs. Wright's house, Mya cooked for everyone. They sat around and looked at photos of the girls growing up. Libra and Mya couldn't believe how much they looked like their mothers. Miracle looked just like Reesie when she was a baby. Libra excused herself and went to her room. She hadn't had any time to grieve, because she had been everyone else's support system. Keke saw the opportunity to be alone with her, and he took it. Knowing that Nutcase was out of town, he had a couple of days to be in her presence. So what if it was only when everyone else was around? Some time was better than no time.

Keke's phone vibrated on his hip, and he looked at the caller ID. It was Sasha. He wanted to build that trust level with her, so he went to the restroom to take the call.

"What's crackin'?" asked Keke.

"Hello Lamar. I wanted to know if you want to catch a movie tonight. I can't get you out of my head. I also wanted to talk to you about something I know you'll be interested to know," Sasha stated on a more serious note.

"Fo' sho, Ma. What time you talkin' 'bout?"

"Now! If a sistah got it like that," said Sasha suggestively.

"Sasha, I'ma call when I'm on my way." With that, they disconnected the call.

Keke notified everyone that he was leaving and told Lorenzo and Gemini what the deal was. Sasha was already outside on her porch waiting when he pulled up in the old school. She looked good to Keke, wearing her red J-Lo sweat suit with some white New Balance tennis shoes and her red Dooney and Burke backpack.

"What cha wanna go see, Shawty?" Keke asked when she was in the car.

"I really don't care. I have some mind-blowing information to share with you. But Keke, what I'm about to tell you can cost me my job, as well as my life."

Keke listened with intensity.

"You see, the reason Pooh's acting strange is because she's seeing that crazy muthafucka' Caelin. She called me a couple of days ago wanting to know if I'd let them see the twins again," Sasha said, holding her head down and picking with her fingers from being nervous.

"Sasha, what the fuck you mean again?" Keke yelled pulling over on Interstate 370.

"Keke, just listen before you start going ballistic on me, please."

"Okay. Go on, man." He turned to face her.

"You see, the day of Reesie's funeral, Pooh and Caelin contacted me and asked me if there was any way I could get them into the hospital to see the twins when none of you were there. For a small fee of course, I agreed. I didn't give them an answer right away, because I was scared, but then he kept pressuring and threatening me. I changed shifts with the twins' nurse. Nicki and I are cool. We went to Missouri College together. I told her I had something to do and she agreed." Keke did not interrupt Sasha. He let her continue.

"They both had on scrubbies, so they blended in perfectly. I was with them the full time. Libra called to check on the babies and when I answered the phone in their room and I wasn't Nicki, I could tell she was dissatisfied. I also had a gut feeling that she would be on her way to the hospital, and I was right. Now, they want me to let them see the babies again," Sasha said apologetically.

172

"Sasha, why didn't you tell me this shit the other day?" Keke replied in anger.

"I wanted to, but I didn't know how. That's why I 'm telling you now. With the babies gone home, we can set them up, Keke. I know what I did was wrong, but I feared for my life. I know it was wrong, and I've also liked you and wanted you to know that I got your back. I'm willing to do anything I can to help you," Sasha said honestly.

Keke wanted to slaughter her right then and there, but he knew Caelin didn't mean anyone any good, and before he made any drastic decisions, he could work this in his favor. He also knew Sasha and Pooh had been friends a long time, and if anybody knew anything about Pooh, it was Sasha. Keke had a strong sense that Sasha was sincere, and he decided to take her up on her offer. He had the perfect plan. Well, at lease he thought he did.

He and Sasha discussed their plans, but he wouldn't finalize them until he'd spoken with Lorenzo and Gemini.

Chapter 24

Revenge Is Best Served Cold!

Keke had been tying to contact Pooh, but he had been unsuccessful since the last time they talked. He decided to pay her a visit. He used his key, which he had never gotten rid of. He still owned the house, but he never put her out once they separated. Pooh was shocked to see Keke entering the house. When he was in, Pooh thought she'd seen a ghost.

"Hi baby," Pooh mustered.

"What's crackin', Pooh? You're expecting company or sumthin'?" Keke implied.

"Naw, baby. I was on my way out. I got sumthin' I need to handle. You can wait for me here. It won't take long, I'll be back shortly," Pooh said to Keke in a rush, grabbing her Gucci purse and keys off the kitchen counter.

"Slow down, girl," Keke said, reaching for Pooh and pulling her by her waist. "I want you to know that I'm ready to come back home. I know you've been waitin' on this, and I also know yo' life don't revolve around me. Go 'head. I'll be here when you get back."

Pooh didn't respond to Keke. She said okay and went out the door. Keke knew something stank, so he would have Sasha follow her.

When Pooh left the house, Keke called Sasha and told her to stay on her.

"Baby, don't give her any indication that she's being followed, but stay on her," Keke said, giving Sasha orders.

Sasha followed Pooh to the Red Roof Inn Hotel on Dunn Road in Hazelwood. Sasha called Keke and made him knowledgeable about her whereabouts.

Keke told her, "Stay there. Don't move."

Keke phoned Rhonda and asked her if she could give him the name of the person that's occupying the room at the hotel. He gave her the information and she told him that she'd get right back with him. Rhonda phoned him right back within minutes.

Ring, ring!

"What crackin, Rhonda?" Keke said, happy to hear back from her so soon.

"Hey fat head, here's the information you wanted. Lanitra Washington is the name, and the room number is 777," Rhonda informed Keke.

"That's good lookin' out, Ron Ron. Call me if you need anythin', okay," Keke said, pleased with the information Rhonda had disclosed.

Keke called Sasha back and told her he had the information he had been waiting for, and that she could leave now.

Keke didn't want to be there when Pooh arrived. He couldn't stand being in her presence. He told Sasha he would meet her at her house. He called Lorenzo and Gemini and told them what he had found out. They wanted to get on Caelin's heads right then and there, but Keke said they had to sit on him a minute and come up with a master plan to bump that fool off. The guys listened to reason.

When Pooh entered the hotel room, Caelin was getting out of the shower. Water was dripping from his body, and every time he moved, Pooh eyes moved with his body.

"Baby, I need to talk to you," Pooh said, walking over to Caelin and giving him a wet kiss while rubbing his black wavy hair. Caelin looked at Pooh but didn't say a word, so Pooh continued.

"Keke wants to move back home, and I want him to," Pooh stated frightened.

"I want him to move back in, too. That way, I can keep an eye on that buster. Ya can let me know every move he makes. I wanna know when that nigga shit, shave and bath, ya got that Pooh? Now c'mon so we can go see the twins," Caelin said, putting on his white T, French cut creased Guess jeans and white Air Force Ones.

"That's another thing. Sasha's not workin' today. She said we could come tomorrow."

Pooh was getting tired of Caelin shit, and she wanted out, but it was too late to turn around. She couldn't tell Caelin how she really felt, because he would have felt like she'd betrayed him, and he'd kill her.

"Well come over here and suck my dick," Caelin demanded. Pooh did as he instructed. "Pooh did I tell ya, we goin' to New York in a couple days, so get ready, 'cuz I'ma need ya to drive."

"Okay, Caelin just let me know when you're ready. You know I'm wit', you baby," Pooh responded.

New York City

Nutcase had been out of town because his basketball team had a tournament. The Young Futures won every game they played. He had the best two point guards a team could ask for. They were like Jason Kidd and

Ghetto Luv

Dewayne Wade on the court. Man was number 5 and Ice
Man was number 3. Them boys got game. After the
victory, Nutcase took the team to the mall and purchased
everyone a pair Jordan's.

Later that night, Nutcase got together with a
business partner to discuss the situation concerning Caelin.
Aubrey Yates was a prominent black businessman who
owned several clubs, liquor stores and restaurants around
the New York area. He had connections around the United
States; so finding Caelin Ross would not be a problem for
him. They met at Yates's Place.

"Tyron my man, how's it going?" Aubrey said,
walking to Tyron giving him a hug and some dap.

"Aubrey my man, I'm blessed. I see you are, too,"
Tyron said, returning the hug and dap.

"Come on over and have a seat so we can discuss
that business we talked about earlier. What are you
drinking, man?" Aubrey said, happy to see Tyron.

"Let me get some Yak straight and a Bud Light,"
replied Nutcase. Aubrey ordered the same thing. "Man, I
need some help finding this cat named Caelin Ross. They
call him Lay Lay."

Aubrey listened without saying a word. Tyron told
Aubrey all the hideous things he had done and whom he'd
done them to.

"What is it that you want me to do, Tyron? You
know I got your back. To be frankly honest with you, I
know the cat. Rumor has it that he killed his father and his
father's girlfriend. His father and I use to be cool back in
the day. Bones got strung out on that shit and wasn't no
earthly good anymore. He used to be the man, but his son
took over and treated his people like shit. Caelin is on a lot
of people's shit list." Aubrey continued to tell Tyron. "I do
business with him from time to time. As a matter of fact, I

177

spoke to him a week ago and he wants to come here and discuss some property he's interested in."

"When is he coming?" Tyron asked with major interest.

"I'm waiting on him to call and let me know. I should hear something by tomorrow. I'm almost sure he's coming, because he said this business needs to be handled soon, at least by the end of next week," Aubrey said as he finished his drinks.

"I have my basketball team here with me, but I'm taking them home tomorrow, and I will return with my lady and stay as long as I need to, to get that bitch ass nigga," Nutcase implied.

"Call me as soon as you get back in town, Tyron, and as always, it's a pleasure doing business with you. Good luck with the team."

"Same here, Aubrey," Nutcase said, shaking his hand.

And with that Nutcase kept it movin'.

Chapter 25

Every Dog Has Its Day

Mrs. Wright, Libra and Mya were at home with the twins when Libra received a call from Nutcase. She was so happy to hear from him. She missed him terribly. All she could think about was him holding her in his arms.

Ring, ring!

"Hello," Libra said, as she got off the couch and answered the phone.

"Hey baby, how you doing?" Nutcase said in a deep voice.

"I'm blessed, and yo'self, sweetie?"

"I'm so much better since I've heard your voice. How are the twins?"

"They are blessed, also. They went to the clinic today and they are healthy."

"That's good to hear. What about Mya and Mrs. Wright?"

"Baby, everybody is blessed. When are you comin' home? I miss you," Libra said pouting.

"I'll be home tomorrow to bring the team back."

"Oh baby, I forgot to ask you, did ya'll win?"

"Yes! Every game! We smoked these cats," Nutcase said, bragging. "Libra I know this may not be the best time to ask you this, but I want you to come back to New York with me. Before you go giving me excuses, just think about it first. I know you're going to say you don't want to leave the twins 'cause they need you, but baby, I need you too. Just think about it before you say no, okay?" Nutcase expressed to Libra.

179

"Okay Tyron, I'll think about it and give you an answer tomorrow when you get back. I'ma talk it over wit' Ma and Mya first. I love you," Libra said sincerely.

"Girl, its no word to express my love for you. Dream about me when you go to sleep tonight."

"Baby, I'ma try. You know I don't dream," Libra said playfully.

On the Other Side of Town

Keke and Sasha had become inseparable over the past month. Keke finally realized that it was over with him and Libra. He found Sasha to be to his liking. He also realized that she had things going on for herself. She wasn't a knucklehead the way he'd thought she was, and she was down for her man, because she kept him notified of all dealings with Pooh. But lately, there hadn't been any new information.

Keke decided that Lorenzo, Gemini and he would go into the hotel and get Caelin tomorrow. He was tired of waiting on this clown. Keke had been with the fellows all day, planning the retaliation against Caelin and Pooh. He had called Sasha on several occasions but didn't receive an answer. Keke knew she always answered his calls, and that worried him. He attempted to call her one last time before he left Lorenzo's spot, and he still didn't get an answer. He went to her house, because he was supposed to have been there earlier.

When Keke arrived he saw her gray Malibu parked outside. He also noticed that the house was exceedingly dark for her to be inside. Not even a bathroom or kitchen light was on. Because he had stayed the night, he knew she always kept the bathroom light on. Just in case she was asleep, he used the key she'd given him. He didn't want to wake her.

Keke opened the door and turned the living room light on to see his way through the house. He went to the bedroom and turned on the light. He couldn't believe what he was seeing. There was Sasha, lying on her bed, in a sleeping position, in her birthday suit with her head decapitated and her limbs detached from her body. Both arms and legs, and also a few fingers and toes were cut off. The horrible sight made Keke sick to his stomach.

Anger rose up in Keke like the flood in 1993 on the Riverfront in the Lou. After the sickness subsided, Keke found a note with blood on it. It read: *Da Unstoppable*. He balled the note up, threw it on the floor, and walked out the door, saying, "Fuck ridin' on that nigga tomorrow! It's goin' down tonight!"

And with that, he kept it movin'.

At the Hotel

When Keke arrived at the hotel, he waited a few minutes before he got out of the car. He checked his surroundings. With everything looking peaceful, he was about to go to room 777 when he saw Caelin and Pooh coming from the room. He eased back into the dark blue Crown Victorian. Pooh's car wasn't parked far from Keke's.

"I got a bad feelin'," Caelin said to Pooh, as he opened the car door and looked around the parking lot.

"Baby, you're okay," Pooh said, but what she wanted to say was, "Nigga you should have a bad feelin' after what you did to Sasha."

She chose not to. Keke already had his nine cocked.

As Pooh got in the car, she saw Keke coming from behind with his pistol. He put his finger over his lips to silence Pooh. Caelin recognized that all too familiar look, drew his .45 and shot Keke. When Keke fell to the ground, Pooh screamed and began to run to his rescue, but looking at Caelin's face, she couldn't move.

"Bitch, I wish ya would. Ya gon' be lying there wit' that nigga," Caelin vented.

Libra decided she was going to New York with Nutcase, and she actually was excited about the trip. After talking with Mrs. Wright and Mya, she phoned Nutcase.

Ring, ring!

"Hello," Tyron said in a voice that made Libra's pussy wet.

"Hey baby. What are you doin'?" asked Libra excitedly.

"Looking at the … "

Libra cut in and said, "Baby, I'm comin' to New York wit' you, and I know you're lookin' at the news," Libra finished.

"Yes, that's what I'm doing, and I'm glad you accepted. Now, I want you to go to my house and stay there until I get there. I'm getting on my private jet now to come and get you. Don't worry about packing. Just be ready to ride and drop the team off with me. I want to make sure everyone gets home safe, okay?"

"Okay. I love you," Libra responded.

"I love you, too, baby."

With that they disconnected the call and kept it movin'.

Chapter 26

There's No Place Like Home

Nutcase got on his private plane without delay. He reached St. Louis two hours after talking to Libra. She was waiting at the Chesterfield airport with the team's van when they arrived. They had to make two stops. Half of the team was staying at Man's house and the other half at Ice Man's house. On the way to Man's house exiting Interstate 270 at Dunn Road, Libra and Nutcase saw yellow tape at the Red Roof Inn, but quickly discarded it from their minds, thinking nothing of it.

On the Plane

Nutcase catered to Libra's every need. He made her a fruit salad. He also fed it to her. The Dom P was waiting when they arrived. Dinner was served with lemon-baked chicken, baked potatoes with several vegetables and other sides of their choice. Dessert was offered, but Libra declined because she couldn't eat another bite. She thought she was going to sit back and read a book on the short plane ride, but Nutcase had something else in mind.

Following dinner, Nutcase took Libra in his arms and put her head on his chest and they lay there for the rest of trip. Nutcase took Libra to his apartment in Hampton. He never took anyone there. He always said that when he took a woman there, it would be his wife and the mother of his kids.

Libra admired the photos of Nutcase and his two sons. They looked just like him. Searching the room further, Libra's attention went to another photo of Nutcase with a female. She was almost sure it was the boys' mother. They had her features. Nutcase approached Libra from behind, removed the photo from her hand and glanced at it himself. Libra looked at him and could see the hurt he'd experienced from the death of his family.

"Baby, you wanna look at a movie?" Libra asked, trying to ease the mood.

"No, I want to tell you what really happened with my family," Nutcase replied.

"Baby, you don't ..."

Nutcase put his hand up to silence her.

"I know I don't, but I think you should know. You never questioned me, and I know you've heard rumors. I think you should let me tell you, because can't no one tell you better than me. It's my story."

Libra said nothing. She let him continue.

"When I first started in the real estate business, I had one person I trusted with my life. He was my business partner. We'd bought our first piece of property and needed some work done. Well, Quentin was responsible for hiring the workers. He wasn't taking care of business, and I was trying to feed my family. So I started doing the work myself and hired a few guys I knew. We got finished with the houses sooner than we thought we would, and I was ready to sell them and continue to expand. Quentin wasn't ready for that. He said that I got the big head and I wanted to be the boss. I felt like I was doing everything, so I might as well have been. I was doing his part and mines, along with more."

"The workers Quentin hired jived around too much. I was about my paper, so I didn't chitchat with them. They always tried to be friendly with me, but I know realness and I didn't sense that about them. I'm a good judge of character. I also took interest in the change in my homey."

"I took the family out to celebrate, because as you know, that was an even bigger house for us, so her parents moved in with us. I went to put my boys to bed and said their prayers with them, when I heard a gunshot. I had a safe area for my guns all over the house, including my boys' room.

"They never knew anything about it. I went into the hallway and saw a familiar face with a ski mask holding Ebony by the throat, and then I saw a masked man escorting my boys out of their room with a tech nine pointed at their heads. Then I got this ole hater ass nigga sitting on my couch, that eats food at my table and calls himself my boys Godfather. Mr. and Mrs. Reid treated him like a son, and he got the nerves to be pointing a gun at them.

"Libra, at that point I didn't know what to do. Here's a punk that didn't have a pot to piss in or a window to throw it out of. I would have given this nigga the world. He was like a brother to me, and he set me up. His other worker walked my boys over by their mother and grandparents. I came out of a state of shock from the robbers being my partner and best friend. I had become aware of a guy standing behind me with a gun pointed at my head, and at that time it didn't matter to me.

"I asked Q, What's this all about?"

"Shut the fuck up, bitch ass nigga," Q said, hitting me with the gun. "Speak when spoken to. I'm in control right now."

"I said, Q man, you got my family in some bullshit because you want to be in control? Nigga, you can have all this shit in a heartbeat, but let my family go. It's me you want. You said my name. You must be looking for me. Here I go nigga. I was fuming."

"Nigga, I told you to shut the fuck up," Q said to me. "Now don't let me have to tell you again. Where's the muthafuckin' safe, and don't lie."

"I couldn't believe what the fuck I was hearing. I said, 'Q man, money ain't nothin' but a thang. What you tripping for? Nigga, you know if I eat, you eat, too. Don't let these suckers talk that shit to you. You know they don't want to see a nigga come up,' I stated, solid.

"Q said, 'Fuck that, Nutcase. I want it all. If I don't get it soon, everybody's gon' die in this bitch.'

"I could tell Q was serious, and I wasn't going to jeopardize my family for no amount of money. I also knew Q wouldn't let me leave there alive, but I'd rather it was me than my family.

"I had stacks everywhere around the house, and I gave Q the money that he knew I was supposed to be saving. If anything ever happened to me, Ebony and the boys were well taken care of for the rest of their lives.

"I gave Q what he wanted. He thought he was sitting on top of the mountain. After I gave Q the money, he put the gun to my head. Just when I thought he'd pull the trigger, Ebony blew Q's brains out. At that time I was able to retrieve my 45. Ebony and I exited the bedroom, and shots were fired. Ebony went back in the living room with the boys and her parents, and when she got there they weren't there. The three workers and I were having a shootout. I didn't know my boys were in the room. Once the shooting stopped, I was the last man standing, with a bullet in my leg.

"I went to the hospital and had the bullet removed. The medication they gave me made drowsy until I passed out. I woke up to the police reading me my Miranda rights.

"They immediately took me to prison. The lawyer I had only wanted money. I hired the best attorneys money

186

could buy. Every judge I went in front of declined my innocent plea.

"I remembered doing a big closing on a business deal with Aubrey, and I retained information well. Aubrey told me if I ever needed him, he would be there. When doing business with Yates, you're tied for life, so whatever you need will be at your disposal.

"I got in touch with Aubrey and he made it happen. He knew the judge who reopened the case and made the State do an investigation on the bullets, something that should have been done at the beginning. Q's father was a police officer, and he wanted to see me in jail, because he wanted his son to be the man. He never liked me, because he said I was a pretty boy, but he actually hated me because I had it going on and it wasn't drug related.

"Aubrey got me his lawyer, and I was out of prison after five years. The bullets didn't match my gun. I spent five years in prison thinking I'd killed my family. My family was already dead while the shooting was in progress."

"When I was released from prison, I got the insurance policy of one hundred fifty thousand dollars for the family. I promised I'd do something nice to help the community. I opened a recreational center for the kids, to house an after school and a summer programs. It allowed the kids to do all sorts of things. They even took trips."

Nutcase had opened a part of his life he didn't share with no one, but Libra. She was special to him. She had an essence about her that let him knew she's the one. Libra wrapped her arms around Nutcase as he came to the conclusion of the story. She felt his pain at that moment. Libra also felt in her heart that if God allowed her, she would bear this man some kids, as many as he wanted.

"Baby, I don't care what nobody say about you. You treat me well, and that's all that matters," she said. "I know you didn't kill yo' family. Yo' heart is too good. Tyron, never feel you owe me an explanation, 'cause you don't. Boy, you stuck wit' me like Velcro, so when we have problems, we gon' sit here and work it out. I don't care what the problem is, you understand?"

Back in St. Louis

Lorenzo saw he'd missed a few calls from Keke and tried to call back. Keke didn't answer. Gemini missed calls, as well. He'd been trying to call back. No answer. Lorenzo and Gemini didn't feel good about Keke not answering his phone.

"Damn, Lo, nigga wouldn't be callin' like that if nothin' wasn't wrong. I think we should go by Sasha's crib and make sho' everythin's cool. Knowin' that nigga, he wanna ride on that nigga Lay Lay now," Gemini stated.

"Yeah man, that's what I'm thinkin', but let's make sho'," confirmed Lorenzo.

When they arrived, they saw the yellow tape in Sasha's driveway. The next-door neighbors updated them about what they knew. Lorenzo and Gemini went straight to the hotel and saw the same yellow tape, and this time they were hoping it was for Caelin or Pooh—not Keke!

Ring, ring!

"Lorenzo, Keke's been shot. You need to get to the hospital!" Rhonda yelled in the phone.

"I'm on my way now. Ron Ron baby, calm down. What hospital?" Lorenzo mustered as calmly as he could.

"Christian North East."

"We'll see you when we get there," Lorenzo said.

"Man, you don't have to tell me. I heard her," Gemini said shaking his head.

At the hospital, Lorenzo saw an attractive nurse.
"Excuse me," he said. "Can you tell me what room Lamar Larkins is in?"
He asked as politely as he knew how.
"I'm sorry sir, he didn't make it," the nurse said with sorrow.
Gemini fell on his knees and screamed, "Nooo!"
Lorenzo picked Gemini up off his knees. They walked out of the hospital with tears soaking the skin on their faces.
"It's time to Shoeshine nigga!" Lo said to Gemini.

Libra and Nutcase were in bed, enjoying the lovemaking they had going on. Libra never felt so free in her life. Around Nutcase, she could be herself. It wasn't that she wanted to be anybody else, but his element was different, and she loved being in the mist of it all.

The Next Day

Libra woke up to breakfast in bed, steak, eggs, grits, toast, rice and hash browns. Nutcase knew they had business to attend, but he also wanted to make this a pleasant trip. He didn't want to engage a man for the job. He and his woman could get the satisfaction of damaging the person that had brought so much pain to their lives.
"Libra, I have a plan that's going to get Caelin. You have to listen to me and pay real close attention if this is going to work," Nutcase stated with seriousness.
"Tyron, whateva' I have to do to get that bitch, I'm down. If I have to cut his head off, I will. That's how bad I

want him," Libra said frowning and biting her bottom lip with her nostrils flaring.

"Go ahead and eat your food, I'm going to give Aubrey a call and see what the deal is. Be ready to listen when you're finished, okay?" Nutcase commented.

"Okay," Libra said with a mouth full of food.

Ring, ring!

"What's up, Tyron baby," Aubrey asked.

"Same old thing, fam. You have any information about what we talked about yesterday?"

"I received a phone call this morning, and he's on his way. As soon as he gets here, I will give you a call. He's coming with a young lady name Lanitra," Aubrey disclosed.

"Give me a call. I'll be waiting. And thanks a million, man."

Tyron disconnected the call.

Nutcase gave Libra the low-down. He told her exactly what he wanted her to do when the time came to meet face-to-face with the devil. But until he heard back from Aubrey, he figured he would cater to his woman.

Libra was getting dress to spend the day with Nutcase when she looked at her cell phone and noticed a number of missed calls from home. She instantly called home, thinking something was wrong with the twins.

Ring, ring!

"Hello!" Libra said excited.

"Scales, why haven't you been answerin' that damn phone?" Mya bitched.

"It was in my purse on vibrate. What's wrong? Are the twins all right?" Libra asked, not knowing what to think.

"The twins are fine and Ma and me are okay. But what I called to tell you is nothin' very serious. Scales, Keke is dead," Mya whispered into the phone.

"Say what?" Libra asked again.

"Scales, you heard me right the first time."

Mya heard a loud noise in her ear and knew that could mean one of two things. Either Libra dropped the phone or threw it. Nutcase picked up the phone and asked Mya what did she say and she repeated it to Nutcase.

Nutcase felt bad. He didn't wish death on no one, because there wasn't no coming back from that.

"Mya, I'll have her call you when she's more composed," Nutcase assured her.

"Libra, I'm sorry to hear that, baby," Nutcase stated sincerely.

"Tyron, you ready to take me out like you promised?" Libra asked.

"Ready when you are," Nutcase replied.

Caelin called Aubrey to let him know he wasn't far away and he would be arriving soon. He also enlightened Aubrey that he would not be staying as planned. He had other moves to make, and he wanted to do business as soon as he got there. He couldn't wait until tomorrow. Aubrey told him that was fine.

Aubrey phoned Tyron and told him the plan. Things were working out, according to Tyron's plan.

At the Warehouse

Libra waited at the warehouse at the top at the stairs for Caelin and Pooh to arrive. Aubrey Yates had all the

191

paperwork ready in his office, and Nutcase was waiting in position, also.

Caelin and Pooh entered the warehouse. Aubrey showed them the different projects that could be made and how much money can be made. The only thing Caelin saw was greed, and that wasn't going to get him far. When they reached the office to sign the papers, Caelin said he wanted to look in the storage area where Libra was. Aubrey gave him the okay, because they had already worked out a plan for that.

While the paper work was getting done, Pooh walked to the door and locked it. Aubrey opened his desk to take out an envelope for Caelin, and when he lifted his head, Caelin had a gun pointed at his head.

"Mr. Ross, what's the problem? Why do you have a gun pointed at my head?"

"I don't point guns at people heads and don't use 'em. It's just that Pooh is goin' to handle this fo' me," Caelin said with a grin on his face.

They took Aubrey out of the office, into the warehouse and down the stairs to tie him up. Caelin set his gun down and was shot in the right shoulder by Nutcase's tech nine. The impact was so strong that it knocked Caelin to the floor. Pooh started firing shots but didn't know who she was shooting at.

"Muthafuckin' who ya got in this bitch wit' ya?" Pooh asked holding the gun to his dick.

"Nobody. I don't know where that's coming from," Aubrey told Pooh.

Caelin walked around, checking the storage area, when Nutcase came from behind and knocked him in the head with the gun. Caelin fell to the floor, trying to retrieve his gun that had fallen out of his hand. With blood dripping in his eyes, he couldn't focus completely. He knew there was a woman's shadow, but it wasn't Pooh, and that worried him.

"Bitch ass nigga, what you need the gun for?" Libra asked, walking in front of Caelin kicking him in the face with her tennis shoes that she had made just for him. At the bottom of her shoes she had nails sticking from out. Caelin moaned in horrible pain, from the holes in his face with blood dripping from them.

"Bitch ya gon' pay for this. Pooh gon' whip yo' ass like ya stole sumthin'," Caelin shouted to Libra.

"Check this out, guy. Don't yell at my woman," Nutcase said as he tied Caelin to the chair.

They heard Aubrey coming close to where they were standing. He had Pooh by her hair and was dragging her on the floor.

When Aubrey reached the others, he tied Pooh up, also. Pooh looked at Libra with hatred in her eyes.

"Pooh, I wanna ask you a question, woman to woman," Libra said to her.

"Hoe what you want? You one of those pretty bitches that takes women like me men and then you think everybody suppose to base their lives around you. Tell me what you got that I don't. Why couldn't I have Keke all to myself? And now he's dead. Libra, I hate you so much. The only reason why I helped this foolish muthafucka' is because I knew if I hurt yo' friend, that would hurt you."

"Pooh, what the fuck are you talkin' about, hurtin' my friend," Libra asked with her gun pointed at Pooh's face.

"Libra—I mean Scales—that's what she used to call you," Pooh acknowledged with a smirk on her face. "I don't give a damn about nothin' no more. The people I love the most are dead anyway, so there's no need for me to live. That sick son of a bitch over there, made me do things against my will. He took Reesie away from me and then he took Keke away from me," Pooh said in tears.

"Bitch what the fuck you mean, 'Reesie'?" Libra slapped Pooh before she realized it.

"I know you don't wanna hear this, but I'ma let you have it anyway. Caelin use to make me and Reesie fuck. Ol' yeah! We use to get down. Reesie use to say she was straight, but she enjoyed the things I did to her. When Caelin use to spank that ass, I was the first person she ran to. At first I was doing it for the money, but then I enjoyed being with her as much as she loved being with me."

Libra couldn't grasp all this information at once. Knowing she didn't want to hear any more of this foolishness, she shot Pooh in the mouth.

"Bitch, some shit you take to the grave wit' you. That's what they told me. And just for the record, I'm a classy bitch, and I know how to handle mines. That's what you don't have that I have, cunt," Libra said, walking away from Pooh's body.

"Ya can't handle the truth, Scales. Yo' sistah was bumping pussy. If I would'a had Mya long enough she would'a been doin' it, too."

Libra walked away from where Caelin was and went to retrieve a small pickle jar. Nutcase knew that wasn't part of the plan, but he let her do her thing, anyhow. Caelin continued to talk shit, and when Nutcase couldn't take it anymore, he punched him. Aubrey had his clean-up crew to clean the mess. He knew Libra wanted a little time with Caelin alone.

Libra walked back to Caelin with two of Aubrey's men following her. The two men removed Caelin from the chair and put him on a mattress, tied his hands to a pole with him lying on his stomach. Caelin was cursing the men out. He couldn't get loose because they were too strong for him.

"Baby, what you think I should do to this piece of shit?" Libra asked Nutcase.

"Baby, whatever you want to do, but remember to be a dirty, heartless, don't-give-a-fuck bitch!" Nutcase replied.

Libra removed the broom from the corner and inserted it in Caelin's ass. She twisted it around while it remained there. Caelin couldn't imagine ever feeling pain that unbearable. Libra wanted him to suffer like he made her sisters suffer. She retrieved a pair of latex gloves from the table. The two men revisited the room and turned Caelin over on his back.

Caelin didn't know what to expect but he didn't care he would go out like a soldier. He looked Libra in her eyes knowing that this would be his last time seeing her face.

Reaching for his dick, Libra stoked it once. "I know you know how to suck a dick." Caelin spit at Libra. "You know I always wanted to fuck ya and ya knew that, but ya thought ya were too good."

"You couldn't fuck me if my life depended on it." Libra said, cutting his dick off and putting it in the pickle jar. She shot him in the eyes and then two shots to the chest. After Caelin body was limp, Libra removed his dick from the jar and inserted it in his mouth. Libra spit on his body.

She walked away, grabbing Nutcase by the waist saying. "THIS IS WHAT IT IS. NIGGA, SHOE SHINE! NIGGA, SHOE SHINE!"

Libra stopped and gave him a kiss, and with that they kept it movin'.

Chapter 27

Some Things Are Best Left Unsaid

Libra, Mya and Mrs. Wright took the twins to The Science Center. They were crawling and getting into everything. Miracle was her mother all over again, and Chance was another Caelin. They spent as much time as they could with the twins. Lorenzo was the twins' father. He signed the birth certificate.

When they returned home and had put the twins to bed, the three of them crawled up in Mrs. Wright bed and looked at *Soul Food*. They loved family time. Although they were grown, Mrs. Wright never deprived them of that, and she loved it even more when they were grown up. After they finished watching the movie, Libra and Mya were about to leave when Mrs. Wright requested them to stay a minute longer.

"Libra baby, I don't know what went on in New York, and I really don't care, because you look so happy. I'm glad to see you putting your life back together. Now, don't make the foolish mistake you made once. The first time the dog bites you, it's the dog's fault, but the second time the dog bites you, it's your fault. Take it for what it's worth. We can't change the way things happen, but we can make them better."

"Mya, I know you have gone through some things, also, but as you know, prayer changes things. I want you girls to know it's nothing we can't talk about," Mrs. Wright said, reaching for both girls' hands. "Mya I need to tell you something. I don't know how you're going to take the news, but we'll see when I finish." Both Libra and Mya looked at Mrs. Wright, stumped.

196

"What is it, Ma?" Mya questioned her.

"I don't know any other way to tell you this but to tell you, sweetie," Mrs. Wright said, holding Mya's hand. "Caelin Ross Jr. is your brother."

"No! How could that be? He killed my sistah," Mya bellowed, crying.

"Baby, your mom was dating his father. When CR realized that Mia wasn't taking his shit anymore, he killed her. Your mother wasn't aware of his already made family. By the time she found out, you were already born. CR knew she dated other guys, and he couldn't fathom the thought. He wasn't leaving his family, but he made her think he wanted to get back on good terms with her, and then he killed her. We were the only ones that knew about their affair. When I say we, I mean Mia, Linda and myself."

"I didn't tell you because I didn't want you to know about that bad blood. I thank God that you were not bonded with that bad blood. Everything I did, I did it for you, because I love you, so please don't be angry with me," Mrs. Wright said, kissing Mya on her cheek.

"I'm not mad at you, Ma. I wish you hadn't told me. Caelin means nothing to me. The only good thing he has ever done was produce two little people that I love more than life. People used to always say we looked alike, but I never tripped off of it. Scales told me that I look like Caelin, but I thought she was trying to be funny. Now when I think about it, we do favor. I could never be mad at you. I love you," Mya said, giving Mrs. Wright a hug.

As Mrs. Wright hugged Mya, she tearfully whispered, "I love you, too, baby. And you, too, Libra."

Chapter 28

Goodbye

Libra, Mya and Mrs. Wright paid their respects to Keke. Mya also felt she needed to be by Gemini's side, and she was. Libra wanted to be there for Lorenzo, because she couldn't repay him if she tried to for being there for the twins. Libra sang at the funeral and moved the church once more with her perfect voice. Libra had yellow roses delivered to the church. It was packed with them. It was her way of saying "Friends Forever." The roses sat on top of the closed coffin.

Following the funeral, Libra went over to Nutcase's house. Upon arriving, she saw Desha's car parked outside. After parking her car, she used the key Nutcase had given her. Before opening the door she put her ear to it to see what she could hear. She heard nothing, so she entered. When the door opened, Desha jumped off the couch and walked to the door, but to her surprise it was Libra.

"What the fuck are you doin' here, Desha?" Libra asked, fuming.

"I was invited!" Desha screamed.

"Who the fuck invited you to my house?" Libra inquired rolling her eyes pointing to herself.

"And when did this become your house, Missy?" Desha asked with her hands on her hips.

"Girl, I don't have to explain anythin' to you. Get the fuck outta here before you leave in a body bag," Libra stated. Desha walked to the door and Nutcase came in carrying a dozen of red roses.

"For me?" Desha asked, reaching for the roses.

"Hell muthafuckin no! Desha what the fuck are you doing here?" Nutcase asked, looking backward and forward from Libra to Desha.

"I came over here to see if we can recreate our relationship. I didn't know you had gotten back with this tramp," Desha said, looking at Libra.

"Look, Desha, you need to leave, and don't you ever come over my house unannounced. And one more thing. Don't disrespect my lady in her house, because I won't be held responsible for what she may do to you," Nutcase stated. He walked over to the door and opened it for Desha. She exited the house and didn't say a word.

"Pretty, don't be mad at me. I didn't get the locks changed, because I knew it was over with us, not knowing she had a key. Will you forgive me for being stupid?" Nutcase asked, kissing Libra's lips and handing her the roses.

"I forgive you, baby. I know you wouldn't do anythin' to jeopardize me or our relationship," Libra said, kissing him back.

As Libra and Nutcase got comfortable on the couch, they heard glass breaking. Both of them ran to the window. Desha had busted all the windows in Libra's 300 and carved BITCH on the hood, truck and all four doors of the car. Libra looked at Nutcase.

"Tyron, I'm about to spank that ass. That hoe bitch done went too far. It's whateva'."

By the time Libra got her air max tennis shoes on Desha had jetted away from the house.

She had done a number on Libra's car. Libra really didn't give a fuck, because she had insurance, and if she didn't, Nutcase was going to take care of the damages.

Libra went to her trunk to get some music she had been working on. Before she closed the trunk, she saw both of Reesie's Coach duffle bags. She put one on each

shoulder and took them into the house. First, she opened
the black bag. Libra pulled stack after stack of money out
of the bag. Underneath the money was a note that read:

To my sistahs,
Here's a lil sumthin' to make life a little easier.
Ya'll take this money and do sumthin' constructive wit'
it, whateva' ya feel that may be. Scales, what I want you
to do is get that singing career goin' and keep yo' head
up. Mya, I don't know what you wanna do, but make
sure it's positive 'cause you know yo' ass is like the
wind, you blow whereva'. But on the real, ya'll do ya'll,
and take care of Mama and my babies if they live. I love
ya'll, and there will never be any words to describe my
love for ya'll, cause ya'll my sistahs, girl.
Love, Res

Libra couldn't believe she had let the bags stay in
her car all these months and never removed them. She tried
to brace herself before opening the brown bag. Nutcase
wiped the tears from Libra's eyes as she grabbed the other
duffle bag. She opened it. Libra found an insurance policy
on Reesie with a note also that read:

To my babies and Mommy,
I know in my heart that Caelin will not allow me
to live on this earth in peace. He has threatened me on
several occasions. I know in my heart that I will not be
here on earth too much longer. My only wish and
prayer is that God allows my babies to live, and
Mommy, if they do I know you will do everythin' in yo'
will power to raise them like you raised Libra, Mya and
myself. I know I can never repay you, but here's
sumthin' to help you along the years, even though I

know they will never want or need for nothin'.
Love ya'll, Reesie

When Libra finished reading the letter, she removed the contents from the bag. She retrieved two million dollars from the black bag and three million from the brown bag. She was so stunned, she couldn't shed another tear.

"Baby, I need to go so I can tell Ma and Mya about this," Libra whispered to Nutcase.

"Libra, do you need to me go with you? How are you going to get there?" Nutcase asked Libra, and they started laughing.

"Baby, do you know how long these bags been in my car? Maybe if I had paid more attention to Reesie, I would' a saw this comin'," Libra said, blaming herself.

"Libra, you did what a friend would have done. Don't be so hard on yourself, baby." Nutcase held Libra for a while, until she fell asleep in his arms. She drifted off into a dream.

"Ladybug, I love you and I know you love me too. I will, for eternity, be that nigga fo' you."

Libra woke up in a cold sweat but Nutcase was right by her side to help calm her down. Rubbing Libra's back, Nutcase didn't ask any questions because he felt she was still distraught. Nutcase took Libra home to deliver the news about what she'd discovered.

Chapter 29

New Beginnings

"Push, baby, push!"

"I can't! This shit hurt!" Libra yelled on the delivery table.

"Come on, Libra. One more time," Nutcase demanded as he grabbed her hand.

"A healthy baby boy!" the doctor said. "Dad, would you like to cut the cord?"

"Sure!" said Nutcase, taking the instrument from the doctor.

Six Months Later

Libra, Nutcase, Mya and Gemini had a double wedding. The royal and baby blue was good-looking. Mrs. Wright gave the girls away. That was one of the happiest days of her life. Her only wish was that her daughter had been there, but she knew that she was in a better place. Mrs. Wright also knew that she had her grandbabies, and Libra and Mya would always be her daughters.

After the wedding, the couples immediately went on their honeymoon. Jamaica was waiting on them. Mrs. Wright kept Tyron Jr. while they went on their trip. Libra didn't want to leave the babies on Mrs. Wright's shoulders. She thought it would be too much, but Mrs. Wright assured her and she agreed, as did Nutcase.

Gemini and Mya loved each other deeply and dearly. Mya never thought in a million years that she would find a man like Gemini. God really looked beyond her faults and saw her needs when Gemini became a part of her life.

Libra missed the babies terribly and couldn't wait to get home to them. They were only staying a week in Jamaica and then they were going to France. Unfortunately, they didn't make it to France. Mr. John called Libra and Mya and gave them some horrible news that Mrs. Wright had become very sick and was hospitalized. Nutcase got his private jet and the four of them made it back to the Lou in no time flat.

When Libra and Mya arrive at St. Mary's Hospital, Mrs. Wright had expired.

Libra cried out, "Why, God? What did I do? Everything I love, you take away."

Mya grabbed Libra and hugged her tightly, crying also.

"Scales, we gon' get through this. We just got to be strong." She held Libra tighter than before.

Nutcase, Gemini and Lorenzo came to the hospital with the babies. When Libra saw Nutcase with Baby Tyron, she ran to them and hugged both of them for dear life. Then she went and kissed the twins, who were walking now, looking just like Reesie. The tears didn't subside. They continued and became unbearable. Libra looked back at Nutcase.

"Baby, promise me that you will never leave us. Please Tyron. I need to hear those words."

Nutcase looked at his wife and told her everything she needed to hear at that moment. They weren't just words coming out of his mouth. He meant every single one of them as he kissed her and his son on the forehead. Lorenzo sat in the corner with his head in his hands. Gemini held

Mya in his arms. She had his G-Unit shirt soaked with tears.

Even though they all had their own houses, they decided to stay at Mrs. Wright house until the funeral. Lorenzo and Gemini put the twins to bed, and Nutcase did the same for Baby Tyron. Libra and Mya knew that God had blessed them with the best mama in the world. Even though they didn't have their biological mothers, they couldn't have asked for a better mother. They waited on the guys to finish with the babies and went to their rooms. Lorenzo sat in the living room by himself, looking at the photos of Reesie and the watch she had purchased him, wishing he had spent more time with her while she was here. He fell asleep with Reesie's photo on his chest.

Chapter 30

Doing the Right Thing

Libra and Mya knew life had to continue, so they did what was needed. They buried Mrs. Wright next to Reesie. Pictures of each of them were engraved into their tombstones. Lorenzo kept his promise and took care of the twins as if they were his biological children.

Gemini and Mya gave birth to a healthy baby girl on Reesie's birthday. Reesie Denise McClendon was a spitting image of her father. She had the prettiest eyes. Mya nicknamed her Re Re. Mya was ready to go back to work at the restaurant she had opened and named MRL. If Mya couldn't do anything else, she knew how to cook. She served the best soul food in the Lou. The place was always packed. Mya made the place very homely. She had photos of all the prominent black personalities in the Lou. The twins were two years old and loved Nelly and Murphy Lee. Libra had Talent Tuesday. Lil Sam and St. Louis Slim had comedy night on Wednesday. Thursday night was Neo Soul night. Gemini was very proud of his wife for her accomplishments.

Mya went so far as to feed the homeless on a daily basis. The building next to the restaurant became a homeless shelter. Mya never realized how many homeless people were in the city and the country. This just wasn't any homeless shelter. It was for abused women and children. Mya and Gemini were building new homes for the women and children who didn't have any place to stay. The shelter was beautiful. The homeless and abused lived the way Mya and Gemini did.

· This is what Mya decided to do with the money her sister left her. She knew if Reesie were here, she would be proud of her. At night when she went to bed, she looked up to heaven and told Reesie, "This is all for you, kid, 'cause you're my sistah."

Libra was in the studio making demos to send out. She purchased a building in the Soulard area. Ghetto Luv Studios was off the chain. All the local rappers came to make their demos, also. She also opened a daycare center, Unconditional Luv.

Business was booming for her and Mya. The twins lived with Lorenzo, but they all raised them. They grew up as close to their own kids as the three sisters had. Nutcase started coaching Chance and Baby Tyron for basketball. Libra kept Miracle in the music studio with her. She couldn't wait until Re Re got older, because she would be with them, also.

They even had a talent show for the kids to show their talent, and Libra couldn't believe all the talent that was in the Lou. Whoever won, they got a four-year scholarship to the college of their choice and a free demo to send to record producers. Nutcase held tryouts for the basketball team, and he traveled all over the US for tournaments.

Libra and Mya were happy with what they'd done to better the community. Life was better than it had ever been, except for the lost of their mothers and sister. But God had blessed them tremendously.

Printed in the United States
201306BV00001B/1-75/A

9 780975 363430